D1260233

The Greenlee Project

By Amanda M. Thrasher

progressiverisingphoenix.com

Copyright © 2014 Amanda M. Thrasher
All rights reserved.
ISBN: 978-1-944277-03-1
Published 2014 by Progressive Rising Phoenix Press, LLC
Library of Congress Registration Number TX0007885799

www.progressiverisingphoenix.com

Book Design by Kalpart. Visit www.kalpart.com

Cover Photo: BIGSTOCKPHOTO www.bigstockphoto.com

Editor: Anne Dunigan

Editor: Jody Amato

Table of Contents

Chapter 1 - Greenlee

I'd rather be dead than climb those steps! Greenlee thought, staring at the concrete that would lead to her final bout of humiliation. It was a given that life, at least as she knew it, was over! Why had this happened to her? She stared up at the looming dark doors of Aubrey Marcus High School. They were not a very welcoming sight, and despite her best efforts, her feet simply would not move.

Greenlee Lynn Granger by name, designated project by default. A ruined teenager and barely a teenager at that! Fourteen years old, just a normal girl, not one of the beautiful people in high school, but popular enough, if only in her mind. She wasn't as tall as she'd like, but hopeful that she'd have a growth spurt soon. With the usual multicolored wire-wrapped teeth, dishwater blond hair that she couldn't do a thing with, and big brown eyes, Greenlee Granger was just another average girl living in suburbia. Well, until now.

She'd managed to dodge Marianne, her best friend, on the north side of the school. Greenlee wasn't in the mood to talk, not even to her. She sat down on the bottom step of the stairs that led into the school, wrapped her arms around herself, and blinked away the tears that had welled up in her eyes. Wiping her face, she made a split-second decision to leave the school premises. Greenlee gathered up her backpack and the jacket that her mom had insisted she carry, and headed back toward the street. The consequences of this decision never crossed her mind. She left the grounds as quickly as she could. It would merely be a matter of time before the rumors, innuendo, and the never-ending questions were asked, followed by the incessant phone calls. In her heart, Greenlee wasn't ready to face the world. Not yet.

"You have to get it over with, sweetheart. It's your first time back since all of this happened. It will take a little time, but we talked about this, remember?" Greenlee's mom had said that morning.

When her mom's so-called words of wisdom ran through her mind, all she thought was how much they sucked! Her pace picked up as she replayed her mom's unsound advice over again. It wasn't that simple, Greenlee'd tried to explain. This was terrible! Her mom had offered to drive her to school that morning and to discuss her first day back with the principal, but Greenlee had been horrified at her mother's suggestion. The image of her mom walking her down the hallway in front of everyone was too much and Greenlee burst into tears again.

"Seriously," Greenlee had objected. "That's a terrible idea. I can't do that. They'll hate me even more than they already do!" She softened her voice and said, "Mom, just please don't make me go back yet. I don't think I'm quite ready for this. Not yet." But despite her objections, her mom pointed her toward the door.

"You have to do this, you have to be strong and stand up for yourself. Do this for yourself. It's what you wanted." Mrs. Granger had walked over and kissed her daughter on top of her head.

"Greenlee, you've come so far. We're so proud of you. You don't realize it yet, but this, baby, it's the last step." She'd hugged her and spun her around toward the door. "Greenlee, this is it, you've got to do this!" her mother had declared.

Greenlee's eyes had been brimming with tears and she could hardly look at her mom. This would be the last and most painful step in this impossible situation that Greenlee would ever take. Her mom's heart had sunk as the tears had streamed down her daughter's face.

"I really, really think I should go with you," her mother had said, but she knew as soon as the words had left her mouth that

Greenlee would object, and she had been right. Greenlee had shaken her head and left for school.

Why her mom didn't allow her to stay home one more day and wallow in self-pity, she didn't really know. Curling up into a ball and shutting out the world was the only thing that appealed to her. Bed—she wanted to go back to bed, and pretend that none of this had ever happened. Greenlee knew that this was impossible. She'd come too far for that. She would have to face them, all of them, and then it would be done.

Students were rushing by her, gesturing and whispering as they headed into school. Greenlee pretended that she didn't hear them, remaining silent. The snickers, stares, and fingerpointing were brutal. She scurried like a mouse, moving as fast as she could through the maze of students. *I'm pathetic*, she thought. *I've become absolutely pathetic!* Realizing that she had nowhere to go, she continued to place one foot in front of the other, with no particular destination in mind. Digging her hands deep into her jean pockets, she felt a crisp dollar bill that she'd forgotten about. Greenlee bent down and rummaged through her backpack. In a tiny zipped-up pocket, she found a crumpled and worn five-dollar bill. She managed to scrape up a few coins as well, with a combined total of just over seven dollars for bus fare. Pulling her pink hoodie up to cover her face, she walked down the street. Her phone rang a familiar tune and made her jump. It was Marianne. Greenlee didn't answer it. She didn't want to talk to her friend, certainly not at this moment. Then the familiar beep indicated that a voice-mail message was waiting. Surprising even herself, Greenlee deleted the message without listening to it. Tears welled up in her eyes again. She wiped them away with her sleeve, took a deep breath, and continued down the street.

Chapter 2 - Marianne

Marianne hit redial for the third time and it went straight to voice-mail. It was clear that Greenlee didn't want to talk. Marianne left one last message, stressing that she was worried about her friend. She set her cell phone to vibrate and slid it into her pocket instead of her backpack. School rules aside, Marianne had made up her mind that she would answer her phone if Greenlee called. Marianne hated her English class and despised it even more now that Greenlee wasn't there. Why hadn't Greenlee answered her phone? Where was she? Marianne knew she couldn't call Greenlee's house. That would send up red flags that Greenlee wasn't at school. She'd just have to wait it out. Anxiously Marianne brushed her fingers over her phone; still nothing.

"Hey, where's Greenlee?"

Marianne turned around in her chair and glanced over her shoulder toward Eric. She thought that Eric was cute, not great looking, but cute. Her cheeks flushed as she struggled to think of something believable to say. He was staring at her, but the look on his face wasn't sincere. He didn't care about Greenlee or where she was. He was just being nosy. Marianne didn't know where Greenlee was, and that was the truth. She said the first thing that popped in her head.

"She's sick."

"Yeah, right! Whatever!" he said snidely. Marianne couldn't help but notice that he immediately turned toward a group of boys sitting in the corner, all of whom were waiting for an answer from him. He nodded smugly in their direction and chortled. All the boys began to laugh as well.

"You're such a moron," Marianne said in defense of her best friend, who wasn't present to stand up for herself. "Grow up already." She raised her hand to give them the finger but stopped midway when she realized that all eyes were on her. The English teacher rose up in full view, which forced her to lower her hand. She glared at Eric, eyes like daggers, warning him to back off. He scowled back at her, laughed, and turned away. The boys cut up, shoving each other as they checked their phones for new messages.

Marianne's mind flashed back to what had happened to Greenlee, and she felt sick. Her immediate thoughts were with Greenlee. Once again she slipped her hand into her pocket to check her phone; still nothing. No missed calls, no voice-mail, no text. What was Greenlee thinking?

Marianne texted: **RU OK?**

She didn't expect Greenlee to respond, but stared at her phone just in case she did. She slid the phone back into her pocket and tried to focus on what the teacher was discussing. She wondered if something else had happened to Greenlee that she didn't know about. She hoped not. Marianne forced that thought out of her head, and wrote fake notes in her notebook so she wouldn't draw attention to herself. She was worried and couldn't focus, but didn't know what else to do. For a split second she wondered again if she should call Greenlee's house. No! She pushed that thought right out of her head. That was the last thing that Greenlee needed. Time, she just needed some time. With any luck, things would seem different by tomorrow morning, or at least Marianne hoped so.

The bell finally rang, but not soon enough for Marianne. She rushed out the door and down the hallway, eager to get to her locker. Marianne pulled out her phone and texted Greenlee one more time.

Marianne texted: **Girl, you're freaking me out. Call or text.**

She hit send and stared at the phone. Marianne was starting to feel a tinge of anger surge through her body over this whole thing.

As she headed to science class, she navigated a path through the open-mouthed and staring students who surrounded her. Marianne wanted to avoid as many people as possible. Most kids had enough tact to say nothing, with the exception of Brittany, Laurel, and Kelsey.

"Is Greenlee around?" Laurel asked. "I need help with a *project*."

The three girls laughed.

"Good one," Brittany replied, adding, "maybe she could help me too, with my new *project*."

Marianne didn't respond. If she did, ugly wouldn't begin to define how she'd react to the cruel words of the girls standing before her.

"Hey, tell Greenlee we're really sorry the *project* wasn't completed in a timely manner. If it had been, maybe this wouldn't have happened. I mean, it wouldn't have gotten this bad, you know what I mean?" Brittany said, glancing at Laurel and Kelsey, seeking approval of her last snide comment. The girls covered their mouths, rolled their eyes, and walked away laughing and making fun of a girl who wasn't even present to defend herself.

"Brittany, you're pathetic. You absolutely suck! Oh, did I say that? Why yes, I think I did," Marianne yelled down the hallway at her, but none of the girls turned around.

Chapter 3 - There's Nothing Wrong

Greenlee sat down on the concrete bench at the bus stop. She had no idea where the next bus was going, but she knew she was getting on it. Holding her backpack on her lap, she laid her head on top of it. When the bus came around the corner, she realized that her options were limited. She could either go back to school and face her peers, although not likely, or get on the bus and go wherever it took her. Greenlee didn't want to see her mother or have her escort her back to school, which she knew she would do.

The bus seemed like the only logical option left. She had no idea where she was going and the bus would simply end up taking her somewhere, anywhere else but here. As the bus slowed to a stop, the exhaust fumes engulfed her. She blinked and shook her head from side to side, coughing and covering her mouth with her sleeve. She hadn't noticed that there were other people waiting to board the bus, and she suddenly felt panicked and hoped that no one would recognize her.

Greenlee pulled her five-dollar bill out of her pocket and handed it to the bus driver as she climbed aboard. The bus driver stared at her as if she had forgotten something or hadn't handed her enough money.

"Where are you going, dear?" a lady asked from behind her. "The driver needs to know if you want a one-way ticket or a day pass. And the machine doesn't make change." The lady half smiled and nodded toward the bus driver, prompting Greenlee to speak to her and tell her what she needed.

Greenlee forced a smile as she looked at the bus driver. She had no idea what to tell her. She didn't know where she was going or where she wanted to get off. She usually walked everywhere she went or her parents would drive her. She wasn't familiar with the bus system and she began to panic, turning bright red, as it occurred to her that she was holding up the line for everyone else.

"One way, please," she said hoping no one realized that she had no idea where she was headed.

"That's too much money. Do you have any coins?" the bus driver asked, tapping a screen in front of her with one hand and glossing her lips with the other. Greenlee showed her the coins and the driver said, "Put in a dollar fifty." Greenlee did. "Do you want a transfer?" She nodded as if she knew exactly what that was, although she didn't. As the driver handed Greenlee the transfer ticket, the older lady who stood behind her asked her a question that took her by surprise and she wasn't prepared to answer. "Are you okay, dear?"

Greenlee wasn't okay. She was anything but okay. Her heart sank as she forced a smile and pretended that all was well.

"I'm fine," she said. "Thank you for asking."

She had lied to a stranger to protect herself from the truth. Everything was wrong. Her life was over; she was sure of it, but how could she possibly go back now? She thought it had been handled, that it was finished, but was it, really?

The middle of the bus seemed like the perfect spot to appear less conspicuous to random strangers. Greenlee sat next to the window and placed her backpack beside her. A rumbling stomach reminded her that she hadn't eaten yet. Glancing at her phone, she saw it was already nine-forty; no wonder she was starving. She had been up since five-thirty. Each time the bus stopped, she observed the people getting off and on, making a mental note of the particular stops they had made. Useless information she would never need, but it kept her mind busy. She kept reverting to the events that had taken place hours before. Abject public humiliation had been too much for her. Blinking away the tears that filled her eyes, refusing to let them fall, Greenlee watched the kind lady who had helped her as the lady stepped off the bus and walked away.

The bus pulled slowly away from the stop, and Greenlee closed her eyes. Her mind drifted backward. *Laughter.* She heard the laughter of the others ringing through her head, and saw the fingerpointing of her peers flash through her mind. She opened her eyes and stared out the bus window. Her cheeks were burning, flushed with embarrassment. How could she have been so stupid? How was it that she hadn't known? She lay down in the seat and sobbed, and before she knew it, drifted off to sleep. It would have been better if she'd stayed awake. In her dream, she went back to the beginning of her nightmare.

Chapter 4 - Star Gazing

"OMG, look at that!" Marianne squealed, shoving Greenlee playfully into Audrey. "Is he cute or what?"

Greenlee and the others stared at the object of Marianne's claims, and yep, sure enough, the new kid was even better than that. He was hot! Laurel and her crew would be all over him in a matter of time, that was for sure, and everyone standing around Greenlee knew it.

"How come guys like that never look at girls like us?" Marianne asked no one in particular, never once taking her eyes off him.

"Speak for yourself," Audrey replied. "I'm a goddess, a true boy magnet, and I'm sticking with it. I'm sure it's working because he just checked me out!" Audrey giggled and the other girls laughed as they continued to watch the new guy make his way down the hall.

"He's beautiful," Greenlee stated. "All the girls stare at him like they're watching a movie star, a model, or something. Sounds stupid, but look at them checking him out. I'm doing it and I feel like an idiot because I can't seem to help myself. Speak of the devil and look who's moving in!"

The girls knew exactly what she meant and continued to watch him talk with the other guys at the lockers. Laurel and her crew slithered closer to the boys.

"He's got to be an athlete. Of course that won't hurt his popularity," Caroline added.

Tall and dark with broad shoulders, he was impressive. The girls thought that he had brown eyes, but they couldn't be sure. Not from this distance.

Greenlee tried to stare without being obvious, to stare without staring; it wasn't easy. For a split second, Clay looked in her direction, and she almost died. Horrified, she squatted down and acted as if she'd dropped her pen. When she stood up, they were standing right in front of him: Laurel, Brittany, and Kelsey. Most of the kids in school called them the BP, short for the *Beautiful People*. The BP were laughing and flirting with him. Greenlee and her friends overheard them offering to escort Clay to class. *Whatever*, Greenlee thought.

"We wouldn't want you to be marked tardy on your first day 'cause you couldn't find your class," Laurel announced loudly.

"OMG, that is so stupid," said Marianne.

"He was already popular, but now that Laurel has tagged him, he'll be untouchable. It's so not fair!" scoffed Audrey.

The other guys had seen Laurel at work before and nodded their heads in appreciation of this girl's work. Girls rarely had it that easy. Being the new guy usually sucked, but this dude had it made.

"*Please*," Sarah scoffed, dragging out her words. "*As if.*"

Greenlee smirked, "What do you mean *as if*? Of course as if . . . "

The girls laughed, knowing Greenlee was right. Laurel was beautiful, just like Clay. In fact all three of those girls had good looks going for them, the very reason they were called BP in the first place. They'd be like the perfect couple already, enough to make any awkward teenager feel insecure.

Laurel always looked like she'd just stepped out of *Vogue* magazine. She had long dark hair, always perfectly styled, stunning green eyes, and a gift for flawless makeup. Then there was Brittany, who was as a cute as a button, as Greenlee's mother would say, with her mid-length brown hair and blue eyes. Last, there was Kelsey, whose long blond hair and blue eyes enhanced her classic features. No ugly girls in the BP group: they were perfect. They set the standard for popular. They weren't always nice, but no one ever said anything against them. Well, not in public anyway. Greenlee never had a chance.

"Must suck to be them!" Audrey said. "Right?" She smirked and the girls giggled.

"Yeah, right!" replied Marianne.

Entering the classroom, the girls sat down just as the bell rang. Biology class wasn't bad, it just wasn't fun. Marianne passed around a package of gum and each girl took a piece. Greenlee suddenly gasped.

"OMG!"

Clay had just walked into the classroom and sat down two tables in front of them. He was so confident. Not nervous at all. In fact, all of the guys acknowledged the new alpha dog with a nod of the head, and Greenlee still didn't know some of the kids in this class.

"This class has potential after all," whispered Greenlee.

Laurel glanced over her shoulder and gave Greenlee, Marianne, Audrey, and Caroline a once-over. She turned back around without saying a word. Marianne started to say something but she noticed Greenlee shaking her head at her.

"Just don't, Marianne. She's not worth it," Greenlee said under her breath. "It'll be a long school year if we have trouble with them now. Just ignore her."

Though she didn't agree, Marianne bit her tongue. The thought of being dismissed by Laurel with a quick glance rubbed her the wrong way. Who did Laurel think she was, anyway? Caroline rolled her eyes and shook her head as she pointed toward Laurel and shrugged her shoulders. Marianne pulled out her spiral notebook and wrote down "seriously?" and flashed it at Greenlee.

Mr. O'Brien always started his class with a lecture, then the lab, followed by the homework assignment. Greenlee tried to stare without staring across the room at Clay, but Audrey saw her. Evidently she wasn't doing a very good job of being inconspicuous. She made a mental note to work on that. Focusing wasn't easy. This class was boring and he was so cute.

Mr. O'Brien asked Clay a question. "Mr. Monning, how's your first day going so far? Welcome to Aubrey Marcus High School. I've heard good things about you from Coach Wilson."

Clay graciously stood up from the lab table and thanked Mr. O'Brien. He indicated that he was glad to be among the fine teachers and students of this institution. Marianne rolled her eyes at this display. *He's unbelievable*, she thought.

Marianne slipped Greenlee a note: ***Do you want to come over after school and study? We can do our homework together? LOL JK . . . Homework, right!***

Marianne had medium-length, unruly brown hair with steel-blue eyes. She was skinny but ate all the time and Greenlee often wondered how on earth she managed to eat so much without gaining an ounce. Her confidence was something that Greenlee wished that she had. It didn't seem to matter what Marianne said or did, she was funny and interesting and made good grades on top of that. Most importantly, she was Greenlee's BFF and Greenlee loved to hang out with her. Greenlee wrote ***K*** on the note and passed it back to her.

Still having difficulty concentrating, Greenlee called science class quits, at least in her head. She'd play catch-up later and borrow Audrey's notes, since they were always accurate. Greenlee watched as Clay played with his pen, rolling it around his fingers. For some reason she couldn't take her eyes off him. She wondered if he was listening to Mr. O'Brien. Or was he just bored out of his mind, too? It really didn't matter, anyway. Why was she so easily distracted these days? Crazy, she thought, and kept watching Clay play with the pen.

She scribbled down a scientific term that she didn't recognize, figuring since Mr. O'Brien had said it, she would need it for something. She'd look it up later. He announced that the class could work in groups for the last fifteen minutes, as long as they were quiet. Laurel immediately made her way to Clay's table, sat down next to him, and started talking. For some unknown reason, this irritated Greenlee. *Laurel was so obvious*, Greenlee thought. *Oh, whatever!*

Laurel was whispering and Clay was smiling. The whole thing was kinda nauseating. The other boys across the table nodded in approval, which didn't help Greenlee at all. Laurel smiled coyly at the other boys from time to time, too. She was playing them all. Clay was one of them, after all.

"Look at that: she's totally obvious," Marianne muttered under her breath.

Greenlee nodded and rolled her eyes. "So obvious, right?"

Laurel was smiling and pointing to something in the biology textbook, talking with her hands, and Clay was acting as if he was listening. Oh, surely not.

"OMG . . . she can read! I know that was mean, sorry," Marianne whispered, but couldn't resist adding, "Oh please, you know that girl has no idea what O'Brien is discussing. She's faking it!"

The girls giggled and received a dirty look from Mr. O'Brien. This they assumed was for talking and disturbing class, but then noticed the dirty looks from everyone, including Clay Monning. Laurel's sparkling green eyes were daggers.

Clay turned back around and smiled sweetly at Laurel, who smiled broadly and turned to face the chalkboard at the front of the class. She was so fake. Couldn't he see that? *Well*, thought Greenlee, *evidently not*.

Chapter 5 – Clay Monning

If there was ever a kid who was destined to succeed, then one would have to say it was Clay Monning. It was impossible to dispute this. His parents had set up an infrastructure within their household to pursue this idea of perfection. Tutors, trainers, and even a nutritionist visited their home on a weekly basis to fulfill this goal. It was incontrovertible that his parents would do anything and everything possible to ensure his success, whether Clay wanted it or not. Moving to a new school, disrupting Clay's schedule: not in their plans. They would wait and tell him once they knew for sure a move was inevitable. For now, they'd hold off mentioning it and focus on what they knew: training, conditioning, and football.

"Athletes have to step it up, take better care of themselves than just regular kids. You know that, right? To get a scholarship, you have to be better than the rest. A step above average won't cut it. Do you understand?" said Clay's dad, trying to motivate and inspire his son.

"Son, put that down. No soda, no sugar. Marjorie, who brought soda into this house? Have we not had this discussion a million times? It's addictive and just plain bad for him," his dad said, sounding like a drill instructor.

"Really? Again?" said Claudia, Clay's sister, sarcastically defending the one can of soda that sat on the kitchen countertop.

"It's one soda, Dad. *One.* I bought it last night on my way home. OMG, chill already!"

Clay made an obscene gesture with his hand at Claudia, egging her on. He nodded his head, agreeing with dad, although not really. Watching his sister get jumped on was always worth it. Claudia picked up a football and aimed it specifically at his head. She wasn't laughing.

"You're such a girl, Clay!" she said, frustrated as Clay tried to grab the ball back from her. Quite frankly, the constant Clay façade irritated her. He wasn't perfect and why they pretended that he was got on Claudia's last nerve. He was, in her opinion, a sneaky troublemaker who was spoiled rotten. He was just a childish brat. She actually felt sorry for him every now and then, with this never-ending charade and having to pretend to be perfect 24/7. Just trying to please the parental units was getting old. But that didn't give him the right to be a jerk, Claudia thought. Had anybody ever actually asked Clay what he wanted? Claudia often wondered about that, but knew it didn't matter anyway. His dad wanted him to play football, so he played football. End of story.

The Clay-on-a-pedestal show was performed for family, friends, and the community at large. It was pathetic in Claudia's eyes, but exhausting in his. Everybody expected something from Clay. He couldn't possibly begin to be himself because if he did, he would surely be a huge disappointment. Anything less than perfect was not acceptable where Clay was concerned.

"You moron," Clay said roughly to Claudia as he grabbed for the ball. "Give me back the ball now, Claudia." He had a game the next day, so the no-stress pregame rule of the house was in effect. Sometimes it was good to be *the golden boy*!

The Fighting Eagles had been the state champions three times, and they were about to go to the playoffs for the umpteenth time. Clay snatched the ball out of Claudia's hand, jumped over the back of the couch, and ran up the stairs.

"Clay, you're supposed to be taking it easy. Did you finish your homework?" Marjorie Monning asked him.

"Yes, Mom. Resting now," he said. And no, he hadn't done his homework.

He went straight to his closet and rummaged through his secret stash box. The candy bar was melting and the soda was warm at best. A long fizzy swig burned the back of his throat, and he let out a massive belch. Flopping down on the bed, he shoved the earphones snuggly into his ears. He knew that no one would bang on his door now. Clay closed his eyes and mentally prepared for a game that would take place in less than twenty-four hours. It was a routine he did every week. He visualized as many plays as he could from previous games and replayed locker-room pep talks. He relived the sounds of the stadium as he lay on his bed.

"Play your game, son, do it your way." His dad's words ran through his mind.

"Clay, go out there and make it happen." The coach's words replayed in his ears.

Clay visualized the field, finding an open pocket and just as the ball left his hands, his arm rose off the bed and drew back over his head, utilizing muscle memory. His hand was still wrapped securely around the brown leather ball and he continued to visualize a completed perfect pass. In turn, the receiver made a perfect catch and ran as fast as he could, zigzagging in and out of players. Obstacles on a field suddenly seemed to disperse like pins knocked down by a bowling ball. Clay repeated this visualization process for several minutes until he drifted off to sleep.

In the kitchen, the look on Mr. Monning's face was worried. He looked as if he'd aged ten years when he sat down at the table and pulled out a chair for his wife, indicating that she should sit down as well. Marjorie joined him, her eyes filled with tears. She placed her head in her hands. He waited for her to say something, anything, but she didn't. Rubbing her temples, tears now streaming down her cheeks, she just sat there, devoid of color.

"We have no choice," he said, waiting for her to respond, but she didn't. "We have no choice, we'll have to move. We have to tell the kids," his voice cracked. "Say something, anything."

"What are we going to do?" she finally managed to ask.

He didn't know, he hadn't thought that far ahead. His resume was out and he'd received excellent feedback from a couple of potential companies, but starting over had not been on their list of *to dos*. Moving the kids, especially now, was a daunting idea. Wes Monning was overwhelmed. Marjorie Monning was scared.

"We have to tell them," Marjorie said. "It's only right. They're going to find out anyway."

Wes took a sip of his coffee before he spoke. "I will know by tomorrow if I got the position with Hydro-Electronics. It's a good position. Let's wait till then, and yes, I know it's out of state, but right now, we don't have a choice."

Marjorie's voice quaked, "Our home. Our life. What about the kids? What about Clay and his future? And Claudia, her friends, her boyfriend?" She paused then added, "They'll hate us."

"I can't help that, and I'm sorry," he said as he sipped his coffee. "But we have to eat, we gotta live. Times are tough all over."

Moving was not something the Monnings thought they would ever do again. They lived in a home they loved, a community they adored. Clay was a rising star, an unbelievable athlete. Claudia had lots of friends and a boyfriend. The challenges that were about to unfold were terrifying.

Their families lived close by. What would they think? The list went on and on of the people that they would disappoint. Wes Monning shook his head. He knew that she didn't want this either, but it was clearly out of his hands. He had no idea that when the layoffs hit that his position would be included. He thought that as a supervisor he was safe. In fact, he had overseen many of the layoffs, and as much as he disliked them, he was always grateful when it hadn't been him receiving the dreaded pink slip. It had never once crossed his mind that his job could be in jeopardy.

"It's early in the school year. He's likely to get added to a team, maybe not as a starter, but once they see what he's capable of, trust me, that will change. He will play!" He took another sip of coffee. "Coach says he'll write a letter to the school and to the football coach on his behalf. That can't hurt, can it? It can only help for next season, unless they recognize his true worth before then."

Marjorie shook her head, of course it couldn't hurt but it seemed so little, all things considered. "What about Claudia?" she asked. "It's bad enough being a junior but going into a new school! She's going to hate us. Then there's the boyfriend."

Wes set his coffee cup on the table. "Unfortunately, there's nothing I can do about that. Like I said, we have to live. We have to go where the money is. You agree, right?" The question was rhetorical. The decision had already been agreed upon.

Of course she did. It went without saying that whatever they had to do as a family, they'd do together. They would try their best to make the most of it, despite the objections that may arise from the kids. Marjorie dreaded breaking the news to her daughter just as much as he hated breaking it to his son.

"We'll wait," he said. "We'll tell them tomorrow or even the next day. Let Clay have one more game without worrying. Let him play this last game. He'll need it."

They agreed to wait forty-eight hours before breaking the news that they were selling their house, leaving their home, and starting over.

"We'll wait and we'll tell them together!" Marjorie said.

"Agreed," he replied and his voice cracked ever so slightly.

Chapter 6 - New School

All things considered, the transition to a new town, a new house, and new school had gone better than the Monnings had expected. Once the initial shock had worn off, the kids had been understanding and supportive, a nice surprise for both parents. They had packed incredibly fast, without much time to organize their personal belongings very well. Things had been shoved into boxes with the opportunity to reorganize it all at a later date, Wes Monning had insisted.

The anticipation of a new house, school, and environment had started to kick in, and the anxiety of the unknown had taken over Clay's mind. It was kind of exciting, he thought. Claudia had been relieved; she had actually been ready to break things off with her boyfriend. The timing couldn't have been any better for her. Wes had managed to acquire an increase in pay with a nice bonus. Safe to say, things were looking up for the Monnings.

"Do you know where my box is? I mean the one with my personal stuff in it," Clay asked his mom, who was rummaging through boxes herself.

She stopped what she was doing and looked at a stack of boxes sitting in the living room. "Seriously, son," she said, "you didn't put your name and contents on the box?"

Clay didn't respond. He hadn't marked any of his boxes so there was no point in offering a comeback. His mom wasn't done though. "I told you to do that before you sealed them shut," she said, shaking her head in frustration, and continued rummaging. Clay wasn't in the mood for a lecture; he just wanted his stuff.

The house they'd purchased wasn't bad. It was a tad smaller than their other house, but the yard was actually bigger. Mrs. Monning loved the layout and colors, which pleased Mr. Monning, and Clay, being a gentleman, let Claudia pick her bedroom first. She was shocked but grateful and picked the room closest to the stairs, at the back of the house, because it had a private bathroom. Clay didn't care. His room was tucked away in the corner, next to a full bathroom. He was also right by the attic, which was completely finished and would be great place for hanging out or playing his guitar.

"The first day of school is tomorrow, right? Are you nervous?" Marjorie asked him.

Clay shook his head. Nope. He wasn't nervous. He was excited and ready to meet the coach and his new teammates—potential teammates, he should say. He put his trophies and photos on top of the built-in shelves in his new room, showcasing all of his accomplishments from previous victories. His mom had put together a photo album for him and he flipped through it. Smiling, he reminisced about past games and his friends. His phone rang; it was his best friend Daniel from his old school.

"What's up dude? You don't sound bummed out at all. I guess that's good," said Daniel.

"It's not that bad and the house is kinda cool. I like my room. Dude, the attic is wicked cool for jamming. I can't wait for you to see it," said Clay, still flipping through the photos.

They talked for a bit and got caught up. Hanging up, Clay continued to unpack his room. If his dad and old coach had secured him a walk-on tryout for his new school team, he'd be lucky. It wouldn't be easy, though; he knew that. The team had already been assembled, and they would have been practicing for months. An established, unified team meant that Clay would have to find not only his position on the field, but in the locker room as well. Tossing his football into the air, he wondered what he could do to ensure his position at this new school. Work hard, play hard, and show up for practice every day no matter what. Trying to get on a new team changed everything. He'd been the key player of a team for so long that trying out for a position instead of automatically having one made him uneasy. Clay didn't like feeling like that at all. He felt vulnerable.

Wes Monning walked into Clay's room, glanced around, and then pulled something out from behind his back.

"This will look great on the wall, that one, right there," he said, pointing to the wall behind Clay where the light poured through and framed the opposite wall perfectly.

In his hand was a huge poster of Clay, arm extended, ball in the air, eyes focused as he stared down the field. They both remembered silently what had happened next. Clay had found the perfect pocket and thrown the ball to the receiver. He had caught it expertly. Clay squinted as he read the fine print on the poster: Clay Monning, MVP.

"I remember that one," Clay said with a grin. "Great game!"

"It was a great game, son, and you'll have others." Mr. Monning patted his son on the back. "I was going to take it to work and hang it in my office, but that wall is perfect for this poster. Plus, I thought it was just the motivation you needed. What do you think?"

Clay nodded. "I agree! It'll keep me motivated, all right. I'll get my position back, that's for sure," he said.

"That's my boy!" Wes patted his son on the shoulder.

There was something cool about seeing yourself on a huge poster, especially when everything had gone perfectly that day. Clay's eyes lit up and he walked toward his dad and bear-hugged him as hard as he could.

"That's cool, Dad, even if I do say so myself. Thanks man!"

"You're welcome. Now, do something. Uh, just kidding."

His dad started to speak again, but his tone suddenly became quite serious and Clay knew he had something he was trying to say.

"You know, son, you may have to prove yourself all over again, but I don't want you to worry about that. You hear me?"

Clay nodded.

"Coach said he's already put a word in for you; and though you have to try out for a spot, once these coaches see what you can do, I'm positive that you'll be in!" Wes said, brimming with confidence.

"Dad, it's going be fine. If it's not this year, then it'll be next year for sure," Clay said, almost believing it himself.

His dad listened to his son's wise words, looked down, and grinned. "How'd you get so smart? It must be from your mom," and they both laughed.

Wes continued, "Seriously, I think you'll be fine. I just want you to know that I'm always proud of you, son! Whether you play football or not, it doesn't matter." Then pausing, "Well I might be fibbing a little. I do love to watch you play football, son." Clay laughed too, knowing his dad was serious.

His dad grabbed him, hugged him again, and assured him one more time that he wasn't worried, but he was. He was worried and nervous for his son; he'd worked so hard for all of those years, MVP last season and everything! Clay didn't disappoint, telling his dad that he was excited about proving himself to his future teammates and coaches. His dad felt a wave of pride sweep over him all over again.

"That's the spirit," he said, with a big old grin on his face. "I don't think that even surprises me. Come to think of it, I wouldn't expect anything less from you!" His dad excused himself and Clay cranked the volume up on his iPod, flopped down on his bed, and allowed his mind to drift. Would he be accepted? Of course he would, as if! He'd figure it out, just like he always did! Show up, blow them away, do his thing. It would be fine.

The next day, Claudia and Clay walked down the halls toward the administration office of their new school. Everyone stared at them, but Clay acted as if he didn't notice. Claudia tried to do the same, averting eye contact with strangers. They found the office, where a woman who didn't seem interested in them at all finally acknowledged their presence. Explaining they were the new transfer students, the Monning siblings waited for the lady to hand them their schedules.

"What were your names again?" she asked, proof that she hadn't really been listening. Clay repeated their names, and yes, the school had been expecting them. She handed them each a packet that contained their schedules and a map of the school, welcome them, and sent them on their way.

"That was weird," Clay mumbled.

"You ready?" Claudia asked as Clay examined his schedule.

"I guess," he replied. "You?"

She shook her head. "Who is?"

They agreed to meet at the end of the day outside the office since they both knew where that was. Claudia instructed Clay not to embarrass her; in fact, if he didn't acknowledge her at all that would be just great. He laughed. That would be fine by him.

"Later," he said.

"Later," she replied, and they went their separate ways.

Chapter 7 - Greenlee

The bus pulled away from the curb slowly, but the shift in gear caused such a jolt that it shook Greenlee's whole body and woke her up, leaving her dazed and confused. Her eyes tried to focus on the fabric pattern on the seats. It hadn't registered to Greenlee that she was still on the bus until then. A stale odor wafted through the aisle and filled her nostrils. The smell was nauseating, but brought her back to reality quick enough . . . Greenlee stared out the window with no idea where she was. She didn't recognize a thing. Hanging her head in her hands, she closed her eyes and thought back to the events that had taken place and brought her to this moment.

Cole's laughter had rung in her ears and flashbacks of kids pointing fingers and laughing at her raced once again through her mind. Embarrassed, she sank down in her seat. Her heart burdened and heavy, she knew that she couldn't stay there much longer.

Glancing out the window, Greenlee tried to recognize something, anything, but she realized without a doubt that she was lost. She panicked. Nervously she stood up and moved toward the front of the bus. As if she were invisible, she avoided eye contact and waited for the door to open.

The bus stopped and the doors swished open. Greenlee noticed that the bus driver was staring at her. The woman had an odd look on her face and her mouth opened as if she wanted to say something, but she didn't. Greenlee couldn't discern if the lady was concerned or if she owed her more money. As if purposely biting her tongue, the driver simply shook her head, clenched her mouth shut, and waited for Greenlee to step down. As soon as she did, the doors closed behind her and the bus pulled away.

Greenlee stood on the pavement, not sure which direction she should go. Her phone vibrated and it occurred to her that she hadn't talked to a single person all day. Avoiding people forever was impossible and she knew that, but for now it seemed like a plan. She had twenty-eight missed calls, eleven voice mails and fifty-four texts. Greenlee deleted them all without listening or reading a single one of them. She couldn't deal with it, not right then anyway, even knowing the consequences for what she'd just done. Marianne's intentions were good, but she was becoming a problem with her nonstop calling. The phone vibrated again and against her will, Greenlee answered.

"What's up?" she asked.

"Are you kidding me? What's up? That's all you have to say?" Marianne said angrily.

Greenlee didn't want to talk, let alone argue with her. She already felt like a piece of malleable meat, beat to a pulp for someone else's enjoyment. Regardless of Marianne's intention, being chewed out wasn't her idea of a phone call. Her cell phone pressed against her ear, Greenlee heard the words, but her mind was a million miles away. For the first time the saying *in one ear and out the other* made total sense to her. Marianne kept talking but Greenlee wasn't listening . . . then dead silence. Finally Marianne had caught on.

"Okay, I'm sorry, I admit it. I'm not thinking clearly. I'm worried about you. Are you all right?" Marianne asked softly.

What a stupid question! Of course she wasn't all right. Greenlee didn't respond. Her throat felt as if it was closing up and she couldn't breathe. Who was she kidding? She couldn't have talked through the tears anyway. She wanted to scream into the phone, *"No, you idiot; I'm not all right. I'm anything but all right. I'm a mess. How come you don't know that?"* Keeping her mouth shut, she just listened.

"Greenlee, where are you?"

Greenlee glanced at the street sign above her head and mumbled the name of the street written on the sign above her, adding, "I don't really know where I am. I mean I'm not sure that I really care."

"I can send someone to come and get you," Marianne said quietly.

The comment both surprised and alerted Greenlee to the unusual situation that she now found herself in. She declined. She had mixed feelings about that, wanting to be safe but at the same time not wanting to see or talk to anyone, at least not yet. She knew she faced an impending confrontation with her parents and she was avoiding it. Not for her sake, but for theirs—the humiliation she believed that she had caused them was too much to bear and having not been able to handle it only infuriated her.

"No, thanks. I'll use the GPS and go from there. If I need you, I'll call," Greenlee said calmly.

"Greenlee, I just don't think that's a good idea. Are you sure?"

Marianne was disappointed, realizing that she'd been dismissed.

"Yes, I'm sure. I'll call. Okay?" Greenlee said, knowing that she wasn't going to call her back.

Greenlee was dismissive and Marianne felt ditched. Hurt and disappointed that Greenlee hadn't trusted her, she reminded herself it wasn't about her. Once again she forced the idea of contacting Greenlee's parents out of her head, but had resolved in her mind that if they called her, she'd tell them what she knew. For Greenlee's sake, she wouldn't leave her out there in her mental state by herself.

Greenlee pulled up the GPS on her phone. She was twenty-eight miles from home. How in the heck had that happened? Suddenly she felt fearful and started to panic. She hit speed dial D.

"Greenlee, where in the hell are you? We've been trying to call you all day!" Matt Granger said.

He didn't wait for her to respond and kept firing questions at her one right after the other and immediately Greenlee felt that she'd made a mistake.

"What are you playing at? Where are you? What are you doing?" he asked with a slight hesitation. "Where have you been?" After a pause, he said, "We've been worried sick!" Breathing deeply, he continued, "Greenlee . . . Greenlee, where are you now?"

Greenlee blurted out the first thing that came to mind. "Dad, I don't really know," she said. "And if you don't mind, I really don't want to talk about this right now!"

"You called me," he snapped.

Absolute silence.

Her dad bit his lip, took another deep breath, and as calmly as he possibly could in that particular moment said, "Greenlee, we're definitely going to talk about it; maybe not at this very second, but you can rest assured that we will talk about it!"

"Dad, please, could you just come and get me? Please." Another slight pause and he could hear her exhale, "I don't even know where I am . . . I know you're mad and disappointed in me, but please, can you just come and get me?"

A combination of relief and fear swept over him with such magnitude that he was forced to bat away his own tears. The photo of Greenlee that sat on his desk didn't help: all smiles, sparkling eyes, and freckles across her cute button nose. It took him back to the days when he'd lift her in his arms and swing her around and around until she begged him to stop. He took a deep breath and spoke as softly as he could without breaking down.

"I'm not mad at you, Greenlee," he said softly, "or disappointed in you. Don't say that. But we will talk about this and you know that we will!" He grabbed his jacket and his keys. "I'm on my way. Don't move from that spot and text me the street address."

"Ok"

"Greenlee?"

"Yeah?"

"Don't talk to strangers!" He slammed down the phone and left his office.

As the air chilled, Greenlee realized that she was starving and cold. She wondered if she should ask her dad to stop and grab her a bite to eat, but given the circumstances, she figured it wasn't the best time to ask for a favor. She kept her head down, hoping to avoid eye contact with the people on the street. She wasn't used to being in the city by herself, especially at that hour, and the hustle and bustle of people that spilled onto the concrete made her fearful. Fortunately no one was paying much attention to her, and that brought her some comfort. She shivered as a gust of wind blew through her body. Her hands clambered to grab her sweatshirt and wrap it as tightly around herself as she could. She continued to wait for her dad, who seemed to be taking too long. In less than twenty-four hours she had gone from not wanting to see her dad at all, to feeling relieved that he was finally pulling up to the curb.

The car door opened and she slid into the front seat without saying a word. Her dad asked her if she was hungry and Greenlee nodded gratefully. He pulled into the first fast-food place they came to and he ordered a burger and a large coffee. Handing her the brown soggy bag, he continued driving home.

Greenlee spoke first. Her voice echoed with the sound of distress, her pitch inconsistent, and she frantically tried to compose herself to speak without trembling. It was impossible. Reaching over, he grasped her hand. He never took his eyes off the road and didn't offer any kind words—his simple gesture was enough. It was heartfelt, meaningful, filled with love and compassion, and touched Greenlee beyond any words that he could have chosen anyway. Gently he squeezed her hand in his, and she tried to speak.

"I . . . I can't go back there, Dad, I just can't. I thought I could," she said as the tears flowed uncontrollably down her cheeks. She swallowed, sucked in a gasp of air, exhaled, and tried to continue.

"The whole thing is just too unfreaking believable. I can't wrap my head around it. I still feel so stupid."

She wasn't hungry anymore but took another bite from her half-eaten burger, chewed a moment too long, swallowed, and looked at him as he continued to drive.

"I'm begging you, Dad, please, please don't make me go back there. I still need to do what I'm doing, just maybe somewhere new."

Her words and the tone with which she said them broke his heart. He hurt for her. He was angry for her, angry at himself for not having known, and furious with the kids who were involved. *His daughter! Terrible for anyone's daughter, but it was his daughter.* Swallowing hard, he struggled to find the right words. His voice sounded different than usual: shaky but soft, concerned, but definitely filled with anguish. Greenlee studied his face for a moment but was forced to turn away. Tears had filled her dad's eyes, and though it would have killed him to know, Greenlee felt humiliation engulf her as she realized that she had inadvertently brought her father to tears and caused him such pain.

"It was cruel and I still want to kill him, hurt him, and the others for that matter," Matt Granger said. "And of course I can't kill him. I'm angry, no, make that furious! I'm disgusted and mad at myself for not protecting you." He couldn't look at her, but he had to ask, "Greenlee, how did I not know?"

Greenlee put down the burger and whispered, "It's easy, Dad, I didn't even know!"

He stopped at a red light, released his grip on her hand, and took a sip of coffee. Clearing his throat, he tried to speak again, but he couldn't. The words simply would not come. Rage had taken over and fearful of scaring her, he put his foot on the gas pedal and moved forward into the flow of traffic again.

"If you don't go back, you'll have to transfer. If you transfer, they win. You can't let them win. You are better than they will ever dream of being. I hope you know that. I hope, Greenlee, that you see just how amazing you are. I think you should return to school. I don't know how hard this will be for you. I'd be lying if

I said I did. But I do know this"—he hesitated, choosing his words carefully—"you have to do this; you have to do this for yourself."

He never said another word and Greenlee didn't offer any either, there was no point. The inevitable was around the corner, but how she'd deal with the situation once she went back to school, facing the people who had put her through hell, remained to be seen.

The principal had been calling their house all day long. He didn't mention the calls the school had made to Greenlee.

"We assure you," the principal had said, "if anything else has happened, anything at all, we will handle it appropriately. Any student that may have been involved with this dreadful situation, *if it was brought up again*, will be disciplined to the full extent that the district is able to." He hesitated and added, "Mrs. Granger, you have to know that we do not under any circumstances approve of this behavior."

The principal waited for any assurance that he was handling the situation appropriately, but that affirmation wasn't about to come. Mrs. Granger was angry and her words were sharp and bitter.

"What am I supposed to tell her?" she asked. "That you're handling it as best you can?" She wasn't thinking, just spouting words. "How do I explain that you're *handling* the situation to the *best* of your ability? Greenlee is devastated and rightfully so. She'll never get over this."

"Mrs. Granger, we're trying. We're doing our best."

She despised the sarcasm in her own voice; she tried to bite her tongue, but the poison, the bitter tone toward him, continued to flow, her voice hissing as the words attacked on behalf of her daughter.

"Clearly I'm not thinking straight," she muttered through gritted teeth. "My apologies to you for my tone, but not to those kids, and for that I make no apologies. I can't imagine, as I'm sure you can't, how Greenlee must be feeling right now."

She didn't wait for an answer or say goodbye; she simply hung up the phone and burst into tears. Where was Greenlee? Why hadn't she called? She glanced at the phone, but it still didn't ring.

Chapter 8 - Laurel

"Hurry up and close the door, Kelsey!"

"Rude!" Kelsey mumbled, but immediately shut the bedroom door per Laurel's command. Laurel disappeared into her bathroom. Kelsey's face scrunched up in disgust as the sound from the other side of the door penetrated through the walls. *So gross*! Did Laurel really think they didn't know? Evidently she did, but of course they knew about her disgusting little secret.

Opening the bathroom door, Laurel shot Kelsey a dirty look. "What?" she barked. "What are you looking at? No, don't answer that. I don't care!"

Kelsey sat on Laurel's bed, managing to divert her attention by flipping through a teen magazine and making small talk. She bit her tongue, knowing that now was not the time to discuss what was on her mind—Laurel's problem. Was there ever going to be a good time?

"Check out page sixty-seven, I love that whole outfit. I told my mom I needed those boots!" Laurel said.

Kelsey flipped to the page, and as usual, Laurel was right, they were great boots. Laurel had a knack for combining the right outfit with the perfect accessories. Kelsey could never seem to pull off the right look on her own. Her friends liked pointing it out—"help," they called it, but it often felt like criticism. Kelsey had quit arguing about it a long time ago; easier to go along.

"Those would look so cool with that sweater you just bought and your skinny jeans."

"So right!" Laurel said.

Grabbing the magazine from Kelsey's hands, Laurel turned the pages and pointed to the models that she wished she looked like.

"She's so pretty, look at her. OMG, I wished I looked like her."

Kelsey rolled her eyes, sick of saying the same thing. "You *do* look like her."

Laurel's phone went off. It was a text from Brittany. She read the text, giggled, and showed it to Kelsey. Kelsey giggled too, but she hadn't meant it. The text read, **Joel thinks Laurel is hot.** Laurel wasn't interested, but Kelsey was.

"You're so lucky," Kelsey giggled, acting as if it didn't bother her that the guy she liked thought her friend was cute. Truth was, she hated it. Laurel always got attention. Laurel was beautiful. She had always been slim, but now she was thin—really thin. Kelsey hadn't noticed that Laurel was so skinny. Red flag. *Nah,* Kelsey thought, *they would have known if their friend had a serious problem, right?* She inadvertently looked at Laurel for a second too long, and Laurel caught her. The moment was awkward.

"You freak, what are you staring at?"

Laurel laughed to soften the coarseness of her statement but added, "Seriously, you're freaking me out, Kelsey. Stop it! What's wrong with you?" She half smiled. "For real, why are you staring at me like that?"

Kelsey shook her head and pointed to a layout in the magazine. "It's nothing," she said, continuing to flip through the pages. "Seriously, I was just thinking how much you look like that girl." She pointed to a skinny model and of course Laurel approved.

"How come your hair always looks that good?" Kelsey added.

She glanced downward and avoided eye contact, hoping that Laurel had believed her. She seemed to, and that was a good thing. She wasn't up for a confrontation, especially without backup. Brittany wasn't there and this wasn't a topic she was willing to discuss on her own. Laurel's mom knocked and asked the girls if they needed anything. They didn't. She also held a plate of chocolate chip cookies in her hand and set them down on Laurel's desk.

"I just made these," she winked. "They're your favorite. Kelsey, help yourself and you . . ." she pointed to Laurel ". . . you should eat one or two!"

Laurel rolled her eyes in disgust and waited for her mom to exit her bedroom. "Seriously! That woman is always trying to make me fat!" She pushed the plate of cookies toward Kelsey. "Throw them away!"

Kelsey picked up a cookie and instinctively her hand went straight toward her mouth. Laurel stared at her in disgust and suddenly Kelsey felt ashamed. She wanted that cookie so bad, but laughed and threw it in the trash can.

"Just kidding," said Kelsey.

Laurel pointed toward the plate and Kelsey dumped all of the cookies. She felt terrible for Laurel's mom, who had baked them. She wished that she could have taken them home.

"Man, what a waste!" Kelsey said.

"She's hovering like crazy," Laurel complained. "Seriously, she's trying to make me fat. I don't know why, but she is and it's getting on my last freaking nerve!" Staring at the trash can she added, "Don't feel bad about it. It'll be fine."

"Maybe she's just worried about you. She means well, I'm sure."

"That's a stupid thing to say. Why on earth would you say that? Moving right along then . . . "

Laurel's constant dismissing of Kelsey's comments was humiliating as well as frustrating; yet Kelsey never said a word in retaliation. She did, however, make a mental note of Laurel's defensiveness. She had seemed overly irritated at the mere mention of her weight, and Kelsey wondered if she should be a little concerned too.

"Is Brittany coming over?" Kelsey asked.

"Nah, she's grounded."

They texted back and forth, posted on the Teen2Teen site, and downloaded their favorite music. It was getting late and Kelsey knew it was time for her to head home.

"Any minute they'll be tracking me down," she said, and as if on cue Kelsey received a text. **Time to come home.**

Laurel instructed her to wear skinny jeans and the pink sweater that they liked to school the next day. Kelsey grinned. No problem. It took the guesswork out of the *what am I going to wear to school?* question.

"Later," said Kelsey. "I love that you pick out my wardrobe."

Laurel giggled. "Well somebody has too, you're terrible at it!" She grinned at Kelsey and added "JK!"

Slamming a large bottle of water to fill her stomach and take away hunger pangs that were setting in, Laurel turned on her TV, yelled an obligatory goodnight down the stairs, listened for her parents' response, and then jumped into bed.

Chapter 9 – Team Introductions

Clay took a deep breath, held his head high, and walked through the locker room toward the coach's office. He'd never been so grateful to have his dad at his side. Just knowing he was there gave him the extra courage that he needed. The locker room was cleaner than he'd expected, large and filled with the odor of hard work that had resulted in multiple championships. The school memorabilia that covered the walls were impressive, to say the least, but there was something else about it. Clay couldn't put his finger on it. Individual names and numbers laced each locker door and photographs of players past and present representing the colleges of their choice were plastered around the walls. He realized it was the atmosphere that was noticeably different in this locker room from the locker room in his old school. Success and confidence engulfed the space; no room for doubt. It was a feeling that surrounded them as soon as they walked through the door and Mr. Monning had apparently noticed it as well. He was beaming and Clay could tell how proud his father was. He patted Clay on the back as they walked, then leaned in and whispered.

"This is the one, son, the school where you will shine brighter and be an even bigger star than you already are," he said, grinning.

The boys were watching Clay as he approached, but not by choice. Clearly the coach's orders were indicative of the stares that followed Clay's moves. Slight gestures came his way: a nod here, a nod there, but no words were actually exchanged. Clay walked toward the coach's office, his dad close behind him, and knocked. They waited outside the door, which was partially open. Clay's eyes scanned the coach's office, but as soon as the coach noticed them, he addressed them.

"Clay Monning, come on in." Coach Davis was on the phone and he waved them in. They waited patiently for him to finish his conversation. Clay continued to look around the office. He noticed the shelves of impressive trophies that lined the walls, and all of the photos, team and individual, which had been haphazardly placed all over the walls and desk. He'd stepped over a couple of boxes when he'd entered, jerseys Clay had assumed, but didn't have time to check. It sounded as if the coach was taking a solicitation call, which was sucking up too much time and evidently irritating him. Coach rolled his eyes and cut whoever was on the phone off in mid-sentence. He apologized to the Monnings, stood up, shook Mr. Monning's hand, and then shook Clay's hand. Brushing past them he headed toward the locker room and motioned for them to follow. Mr. Monning once again patted Clay on the back. *A little extra support*, Mr. Monning thought.

Coach Davis was a big guy, and Clay couldn't help but wonder what position he must have played. He wore a polo shirt covered by an oversized sweatshirt, a ball cap, a pair of jeans, and a whistle, which hung around his neck. Mr. Monning proudly said his goodbyes and assured Clay that they would catch up later.

"I take it you're ready to meet the team and get to work?" asked Coach Davis.

Clay nodded. "Yes, sir, I am."

All eyes were on the coach, ignoring Clay. It was an outward sign of unity among the team toward their quarterback. The coach leaned toward Clay and asked if he'd like to say a few words, and to the coach's surprise, Clay accepted.

"I just want to say I'm glad to be here and thankful to be a part of this team. I intend to do my part, and contribute to one of those," Clay said, pointing to a massive championship trophy in the glass display case.

He stepped back and stood behind Coach. No one said anything, though Coach was impressed with the kid's confidence and the way he acknowledged the success of the team.

Coach hesitated for a second, as if choosing his words carefully. The locker room was dead silent. He paced the floor, looked each one of his players in the eye, went back to the front of the room, and in a subdued voice addressed his guys.

"I know you guys have heard a lot about this boy right here," he said, glancing at all the players before him. "But I want to remind all of you that there is no *I* in team!" He had their attention. "No individual is more important or holds a higher position than any other boy on this team at any time. We are equals. Once you hit that field, you boys are all the same, equal in every sense of the word!" He proceeded with caution. "I will . . . we will . . . you will," he paused, "continue to do what's best for this team!"

The boys hollered and clapped, showing their appreciation and approval of what the coach had just said and Clay clapped, too. Coach finished his spiel.

"That said, boys, please welcome Clay Monning to our locker room. He's a great athlete, we're lucky to have him, but he's got to earn his spot."

The boys stared at Coach—Clay stared at the boys. The scene was awkward. Clay realized his palms were sweaty and his nerves felt as if they were bubbling from within, but fortunately they weren't surfacing, obeying a skill that he'd learned on the field.

"Well, you know the rest," Coach said. "Suit up. Go out there and be the men you're supposed to be. Hit the field, boys!"

Clay was instructed to follow the assistant coach, who assigned him his equipment and his locker. He wasn't surprised that his locker was in the far corner, on the bottom level, and hard to open.

"Hurry up; it's time to get to work. See ya on the field," he said and then added, "Oh yeah, and welcome."

Clay got dressed. His pads had a familiar, comfortable feel, and he realized he was ready to get back to football. Normality for him was early-morning workouts, evening scrimmages, and Friday night games. He'd missed it, all of it. He just hadn't realized until the familiar smells, sounds, and feel of everything around him how much he'd missed the locker room and everything football. Finally he grabbed his helmet and rushed toward the door. Frustrated, he found himself standing in the middle of the shower and he realized he'd gone in the wrong direction. He turned around quickly and tripped over a trashcan. Embarrassed, he kicked it. With a quick glance around him to make sure no one had seen, and thankfully they hadn't, Clay headed out to the field.

"I'm certain you studied the playbook that I sent you, right?" Coach asked as Clay ran toward them.

"Yes, sir," Clay responded, and he was relieved that he'd taken the time to study it.

"OK, Golden, let's see what you've got," Coach joshed, and the boys whispered among themselves and laughed.

"Coach just called him 'Golden.'"

As Clay ran onto the field he passed A.J., the current quarterback. A.J. opened his mouth as if he had something to say, but surrounded by his teammates, he held back. Now wasn't the time. He observed the new kid. He was bigger than he'd expected. If he was as good as they kept saying he was, his own position was in jeopardy; at the very least he'd have to share it. He'd been ticked about that possibility as soon as he'd heard about Clay. He couldn't shake the feeling that Coach knew that he was irritated, and it seemed to A.J. that Coach was intentionally promoting the competitiveness between the two quarterbacks, as if wanting to ascertain which one of the boys was strong enough to come out on top. It irritated A.J. that he had to fight for a position that he'd already earned.

"Let's go boys; we don't have all day. Get into formation!" said Coach Davis.

As a show of respect, Clay stopped and asked A.J. a question, doubting that he would answer. It was just an icebreaker, really.

"Anything I need I to know?" Clay asked.

"Yeah . . . keep your head up and don't get in my way," A.J. barked in response.

Coach told Clay the plays and the boys got into formation. The snap was made on the second count. Clay dropped back in the pocket as his eyes scanned the field. His primary receiver was covered; instinctively he looked for his second receiver. He was open. Clay threw the perfect pass and it landed perfectly into the hands of the secondary receiver, who ran it for a first down. *Sweet!* Clay thought.

Great pass, great touch, nice read, Coach thought, but turning to his assistant, said, "We need to work on his footwork."

Clay loved the intensity of the moment, of being under the gun, all eyes watching him. The coldness in teammates' stares reminded him of the situation at hand. If the others made him look incompetent, the position that he hoped to secure would be jeopardized, and their loyalty to A.J. would remain intact. One thing remained. Clay still had undeniable skills on his side. He knew he had to settle down and focus on what he could control, the football. Football was football, and trash talk between the defense and the offense started to take place. Clay knew he could use that to his advantage.

"Footwork, Clay, work on that," Coach hollered from the sidelines.

What? Clay thought. "Yes, sir," he said.

The boys on the defensive line spat out a couple of harsh comments directed toward Clay and then proceeded to go after him as hard as they possibly could, but Clay held his own. He got rid of the ball fast, made smart throws, and only ran when necessary. His guys came through and protected him. Clay knew the reason for that: love of the game, not respect for him, that had triggered the sudden rally around him. Didn't matter, he'd take it. They appeared to be doing their jobs but still feeling him out, still loyal to A.J. but tolerant of him because Coach was watching. He was grateful that they were at least attempting to protect him. It could have been ugly and he knew it. Colton, his receiver, even managed a nod in his direction, a nod of approval. Clay got back into the huddle and called out another play.

A.J. stood on the sidelines, noticeably upset. He didn't hesitate to point out every mistake that Clay made to his teammates and to any coach that would listen. The coaches didn't respond, but his teammates standing on the sidelines with him agreed with everything A.J. said.

"Get out of the huddle quicker; too slow, you should know that," A.J. yelled from the sidelines. "He should know that, really, come on!"

"Easy, son," Coach advised.

Clay's nerves started to act up, but he took a deep breath and pushed them deep down into his gut. *Block it out, do it, block it out, do it*, he told himself, and he did. Sweat ran down his face as he visualized what his next play should look like, and the rest came from within, pure heart, skill, and force.

A.J's teammates, in an attempt to show their loyalty, continued to rally around A.J., agreeing and adding their own negative comments when Clay made a move. Coming down hard on everything he did and every decision he tried to make, the boys started to waver and listen to A.J. instead of what they were supposed to be doing. *A show of loyalty*, Clay thought. Clay shook it off and focused on the plays at hand. He noticed the hits were coming more often and with more force. He continued to listen to Coach. It didn't stop the boys from hitting him as hard they possibly could and trying to teach him a *welcome to our school* lesson. The hits got harder and harder, or so it seemed. *To be expected*, Clay told himself.

"Quit throwing like my grandma. Take what the defense gives you and get the play off. Quit forcing it," Coach hollered across the field. *Great pass*, he actually thought.

Seriously? Clay thought. "Yes, Coach," he said.

The ball snapped and Clay dropped back. He looked up. His tight end was open, but he saw Colton running deep. *Go for it all*, he thought, *or be sure and get the first down*. Suddenly, as if the lights had gone out, Clay realized he'd taken too long. He lay on the ground as the muffled sound of the defense celebrating around him rang in his ears. His blockers stared at him, bewildered or disgusted, he couldn't decipher. He could hear Coach's voice, but couldn't make out a single word. He had been hit by what felt like a Mack Truck, and it may as well have been. Clay couldn't breathe. Trying to stand up, he realized that his head was spinning and his chest felt as if it had been crushed. Sacked; he'd been sacked. Gasping for air, he tried to act as if he wasn't. He wasn't doing a very good job, but when the trainers ran out onto the field to assist, he sent them away.

"I'm okay. I'm good," Clay said.

He had one shot left to redeem himself, one shot left to shine, to make it right and end on a high note, leaving a good first impression with his new team. In the huddle he realized the players thought he'd blamed them for lack of protection. If he was smart, he still had a chance to fix it. A.J. and the other boys were laughing on the sidelines, but Clay focused on what he needed to do to rally his team. It's football—you get hurt. It's part of the game, and he knew that, but unfortunately so did they. Being tough was part of football. Toughen up or don't play; at least that's what his old Coach Wilson had always said. Clay stood up, picked the dirt out of his helmet, and waved to his players to gather around him.

"Let's go, times a-ticking," the assistant yelled.

"OK guys, who's got my back?" The look on his face was sincere and genuine, though from the huddle, nothing but silence and blank stares. You could've heard a pin drop. Clay asked the question again.

"Do you have my back?"

As soon as the words rolled off his tongue, Clay wished they hadn't. But to his surprise the boys' hardened looks softened, and though they never responded, the guys got back into the huddle. Clay gave them the play, broke the huddle, and went back to the line of scrimmage.

"Hut, hut."

Clean snap, that's good, Coach thought as Clay dropped back in the pocket. Clay's eyes scanned the field and found Colton. A great pass from Clay and an amazing catch by Colton. Colton ran like hell and completed the play. Touchdown! Clay's first actual touchdown in his new Raider uniform, even though it was a scrimmage, still counted. Clay knew his dad would have loved it! He couldn't wait to share it with him.

"Oh double Cs, Colton and Clay—if you know what I mean," a player yelled from the field.

Everyone except for A.J. laughed. The rest of the team knuckle-bumped Clay, patted his back and sent nods his way, signs of approval. A.J. walked off the field and headed toward the locker room. Recognizing his quarterback was irritated, Coach didn't stop him.

Clay pulled his helmet off and to his surprise Colton yelled, "Nice pass, golden boy."

Dang, great play! Coach thought. "Gotta take your time, son!" he said. Turning to his assistant, he ordered, "Tell that kid to take his time. He's got plenty of time!"

As soon as practice was over, A.J. requested a meeting with Coach Davis. Knowing what to expect, Coach nodded.

"See you in my office, A.J., but a word of advice—" he paused before going on. "Change that attitude before you knock on my door or don't bother coming in!"

A.J. nodded, turned, and caught up with his teammates. The trash talk back and forth with each other, joking at Clay's expense had started, but Clay didn't seem to care: if they were talking trash, it was a start. A line of communication, even if it was insults passed back and forth, was at least something. The boys hit the showers and nervously A.J. made his way toward Coach's office. He took a deep breath and knocked on the door. He entered and sat down. He opened his mouth to speak, but to his surprise, Coach spoke first.

"A.J., I know why you're here."

Suddenly A.J. wished he wasn't.

"Let me start by saying, son, that I don't make any decisions for my team that aren't for the good of the team." He paused, picked up a football, and tossed it to A.J.

"Great catch; but then again, you're a great player. You're also a great leader, their leader," his head bobbed toward the door, "the leader of this team." He proceeded, though gingerly, reading A.J.'s eyes as if he wasn't sure how firmly he wanted to deliver his advice. "They'll follow your lead, A.J., but you need to listen to me, because I've seen this thing here, what you're about to do, a hundred times."

A.J. was certain that whatever he was about to hear wasn't what he'd hoped. He wanted reassurance that his position was intact, but that didn't appear to be in the picture. He had no choice but to sit and listen.

"How you," and he emphasized the word *you*, "choose to handle this situation with Clay will either help or dismantle our team, and that's up to you."

He tried to decipher whether his star player understood his words. A.J. was listening, but had he heard what he was trying to say?

"Your teammates will choose a side, who to follow, and right now, you have an advantage because you're their current leader. Play your cards right, A.J., and they will follow you." He wasn't quite done, but A.J. wished he were. His words had a slight sting as they hit A.J.'s ears.

"Are you going to let this kid steal your spot and everything you've worked for, including the team's respect? You decide if you want to keep your position and fight for your spot. I know his record and what he's capable of and so do you. He's good; he's a great player, but he hasn't done it here . . . not yet, anyway." Coach took a sip of half-warm coffee and scrunched up his face as if it were difficult to swallow. A.J. knew what he meant. "We're lucky to have both of you. It's a gift having two talented quarterbacks on one team. But you're a senior and their leader. You tell me, A.J., what do you want to do?"

A.J. bowed his chest up. "I want my position; it's mine. I earned it."

"I'd like to tell you that your position is secure, A.J., but it's not. Heck, mine's not, so do you think yours is? This is football; we play to win, not to try and win, and the best players play first. That's what first string is all about. You know that and I know that. So do me a favor . . ."

A.J.'s eyes looked at Coach as he spoke, but his fingers fidgeted with the ball he held in his hands. He was hesitant to answer, doubtful if he wanted to hear anything else this man he admired so much had to say.

"What's that, Coach?"

"Remember this: it's sound advice." He inhaled, and then exhaled. "This position, your position, it's yours to lose. Remember that. It's yours to lose. But that said, this kid can't take it, win it, earn it, whatever, if you maintain the respect of your team and keep doing what you're doing." He picked up his mug again, but set it down without sipping from it. "Keep performing. Maintain the respect of the boys, and of course I have to say this," he smiled.

"What's that, Coach?"

"Keep your grades up."

A.J. grinned at that, but he was nervous. Coach's words weren't exactly comforting and he knew what the new kid was capable of. If he managed to secure a position, it would be his position for sure! He was a proven quarterback and Coach was right: respect from his own teammates would be the key. If Clay gained the respect of his teammates too, the rest would be history. A.J. hated him already.

Coach was done. He held up his hands in order for A.J. to pass him back the ball. "Now go on, get outta here," he said, and A.J. got up to leave.

Chapter 10 - Check the Site

Greenlee soaked in the bathtub longer than she'd realized, and despite topping it off several times with hot water, the water had become cold. Reluctantly she reached for a towel and climbed out. Her reflection in the mirror was distorted, and not once did she consider wiping the steam off the mirror. Staring at her image wasn't appealing. She wouldn't have recognized the person staring back anyway. *No loss there*, she thought. *Who is that girl, the one staring back at me? I don't know her, at least not anymore!*

"Here's a fresh towel if you need one," her mom said softly from the other side of the door. She didn't need one; the linen closet was always available and full. It was an invitation to talk. Her mom, knowing something was wrong, wished she would, but Greenlee wanted to hide. She had nothing to say. All she wanted was to go back to bed, escape, fall asleep, and she didn't care if she ever woke up. Her mom's good intentions were suffocating her.

Putting on her black-and-white plaid flannel pajama bottoms and oversized black sweatshirt made her feel secure. The clothes swallowed her up, allowing her to lose herself in them. She felt unnoticeable and right now that's exactly what she wanted. Her mom was standing in front of the bathroom door when Greenlee opened it. She was worried about her, but Greenlee couldn't look at her. Mrs. Granger grabbed her, pulled her into her arms, and held her close; despite the fact that Greenlee tried to pull away, her mom clung to her for a few minutes. As Greenlee had feared, her emotions flooded over her and she couldn't hold them back any longer. Her tears flowed. She sobbed like a child, once again being comforted in the arms of her mother. Her mom couldn't say a thing that she hadn't already said to Greenlee to make her feel better. Her mom's heart broke right along with her daughter's. Tears streamed down both of her cheeks, though Greenlee didn't see them, being nestled so tightly in her mom's arms. Stroking her daughter's hair and whispering that she loved her, her mother rocked her as they stood in the hallway. Greenlee clung to her mom, shoulders shaking as she sobbed. The tears continued to stream, but for the first time since it had happened, she was glad her mom was there.

The dogs barked as they ran toward the front door, which startled them both. Voices were muffled, but a familiar voice wafted up the stairs. Marianne was on her way up. Mrs. Granger noticed the look of horror on her daughter's face. She didn't want to see or talk to anyone, not even her best friend. She wasn't ready. Her mom squeezed her hand and whispered that it would be all right, adding that Marianne was exactly the person she should spend time with right now, and that she'd feel better after she had. Greenlee wasn't buying it, but it didn't matter: Marianne was almost at the top of the stairs.

"Trust me on this one, please," her mom insisted, trying to convince even herself. "You need to talk to someone and clearly you're not talking to me." She wasn't mad or irritated; she was concerned and disappointed that her daughter didn't want to talk to her. But there was no need to discuss that; she knew enough to know that Greenlee needed to talk to someone. Greenlee just needed someone!

Marianne stood at the top of the stairs; not knowing exactly what to say, she merely held up a sack filled with candy, all of Greenlee's favorites. Greenlee walked into her room and Marianne followed her. Flopping down on the bed, just like she always did, she waited for Greenlee to say something. She didn't. Greenlee was actually glad to see her.

"I know it's a lot of candy, right? I used all of my allowance." Marianne shook the bag, trying to tempt her friend or at least make her smile. "Chocolate, licorice, gum, suckers, you name it, I bought it."

Greenlee looked tired and weak. Fragile, that was it. She looked fragile. How did that happen overnight? Her eyes were swollen, obviously from tears, but she was pale, and the black circles under her eyes looked awful and made her look ill.

"Did you eat today?" Marianne asked. "I mean, do you want me to grab a burger, taco, or something else for you?"

Greenlee shook her head and rummaged through the bag of candy. Settling on a chocolate bar, she broke it into tiny bits and nibbled them one piece at a time. She reminded Marianne of a little mouse from a cartoon, nibbling on a piece of cheese. The silence that had suddenly saturated the room was weird, but necessary, since neither of the girls knew what to say. Greenlee's eyes kept darting toward her desk, to her laptop in its usual place, but as soon as she realized what she was doing, she'd force her eyes downward. It wasn't working. She needed to know, and though she knew she couldn't possibly look at it, Marianne could.

Marianne shook her head, knowing what Greenlee was about to ask of her.

"No way!" Marianne said.

Greenlee begged her. "Please Marianne; I'd do it for you."

"That's crazy Greenlee! Not now. Not yet, wait a few days."

Greenlee couldn't wait. It was eating at her, her mind, her heart, and her stomach. She couldn't stand it.

"I have to see what they're saying. Don't you get that? I would do it for you. I can't believe you won't do it for me." In a quivering voice Greenlee whispered, "I'm not strong enough, Marianne. Not today, not tomorrow, maybe never. But I know you are." She stared at her friend. "You can pull up the site for me. Marianne, will you pull the site up for me?"

"Greenlee, I'm begging you, I'm telling you as a friend, your best friend: it's a bad idea!"

The inability to decide between doing the right thing and doing what her best friend asked brought new meaning to *being caught between a rock and a hard place*. Marianne shook her head and sighed, knowing she was about to make a huge mistake and one she would surely regret later.

"Are you sure? Really, really, really, really sure?" Marianne asked, hoping Greenlee would reconsider.

Greenlee just stared at her. Her laptop was already opened up and she'd put in her password. She was in the process of handing it to Marianne as she shook her head. No reconsidering. The overwhelming urge to check the site had consumed her, and no matter how hard she tried to ignore it, she just couldn't.

Marianne logged into her Teens2Teens site and scanned the page, searching for posts or any thread with Greenlee's name mentioned. Scrolling, still searching. Her face went blank as she scanned the page. Pulling out her phone she checked her inst-a-posts. Nothing.

"What's wrong? Are there more? There are more posts, aren't there?" Panic echoing in her voice, she asked, "What are they saying? OMG. Let me see." Greenlee grabbed at the phone, too scared to look at the laptop. "What else could they possibly be saying?"

"No, wait a minute," Marianne said with an odd tone of her own. "It's not that! Hang on a second."

Greenlee couldn't wait. She finally grabbed the laptop and stared at the screen. Marianne wasn't on the right page. She flashed Marianne a dirty look, but Marianne grabbed the laptop back and continued searching the site.

"Just hang on a minute!"

"Go to *the* page," Greenlee said frantically. "Go to *the* page."

Marianne stopped typing. "That's just it, Greenlee." Her eyes were huge. "There is no page!"

"What are you talking about?"

"There are posts about it, of course, and I'm just being honest, they're not pretty. Nasty, actually, and I don't think it's wise to read them. Just saying: I don't recommend it, but if you want to read those you can." She started scrolling again and if Greenlee wasn't mistaken, she sounded excited.

"Come on already, what is it?"

"Greenlee, *the page* is down!"

"What are you talking about?" Greenlee asked timidly. "Down?"

"The page, Greenlee, *The Greenlee Project* page . . . it's gone!"

Greenlee stared at the screen. Marianne was right. It was gone. Parents were outraged, her parents first and foremost, but there had been others. Clay's request to pull the page, with the help of school administrators, had forced the site to remove the damaging material. They didn't have a choice; someone had to step in and at least do that, and to their credit, they had. Posts referencing the whole thing still clung to other threads, not to mention the infamous video, but the actual *Greenlee Project* page had been removed. Greenlee's cheeks involuntarily flushed beet red just thinking about it. Biggest joke ever played, *The Greenlee Project*, and damn if she wasn't it. Greenlee Lynn Granger . . . *The Greenlee Project!*

Posts:
-Did you hear her say that, so stupid, but he recorded it!
-I know . . . as if . . . really . . . I wonder if he got anything from her?
-Probably, though why would he want to?
-Greenlee, please!
-Where's that voice mail? I want to listen to it.
-It's on Paige's page or it was.
-Headed over there, hahahaha. Lol!
-Dude it's so freaking funny.
-What an idiot!

Marianne's hands were shaking. The sugar hadn't helped, but nerves and adrenaline were racing through her body. She couldn't imagine, if she felt this bad, how Greenlee must be feeling. She didn't dare look at her friend's face. She pretended not to notice when Greenlee's eyes filled with tears and she covered her mouth with her hands.

She read the posts in horror, seeing her name being smeared as they made fun of her. They had been brutal—all of them! Devaluing her thoughts, her reputation, and the relationship that she'd thought she'd had. Poison and filth filled the pages. Posts continued to appear one after the other, as the girls looked on.

Laurel, of course, hadn't held back. The hateful words pierced Greenlee like a hot poker, as they scarred her in full view of everyone. Each vicious word became imprinted in Greenlee's mind, but still she kept reading them over and over again, as if they would somehow change, but to her dismay they hadn't. The nasty comments kept coming:

-Greenlee deserves it for being so stupid!
-Really . . . everybody knew.
-How come she didn't?
-As if . . . please, how embarrassing. I'd die if that were me!
-In her dreams, actually, lol, didn't she say she felt like she was dreaming?
-Newsflash, Greenlee, dip-wad, wake up!
-Did you hear the vm?
-OMG—No—Where is it?
-Frankie has it on his page.
-The whole message, it's hilarious.
-Let me listen. Make sure you repost it!
-Will do!

"OMG, what conversation are they talking about? What did I say?" Greenlee grabbed her phone, but there was no point; she wasn't going to call him anyway.

"What did I say to him and why did he share it? Marianne, why did he do this to me?"

Greenlee felt as if she couldn't breathe. Her face flushed and she gasped for air. Her sweatshirt suddenly felt too heavy. It was confining and hot, and beads of sweat formed on her brow. She ripped the shirt off and threw it down in a crumpled pile on her bedroom floor. She was completely numb. Marianne closed the laptop and sat down next to her. Greenlee was shaking, shivering, and Marianne wrapped the sweatshirt she'd just taken off around her shoulders.

"It was too soon, Greenlee, it wasn't time. I'm so sorry." She put her arm around her friend. "I shouldn't have done that, not even for you. I should have told you no."

Greenlee grasped her friend's hand in hers, but no matter how hard she tried, she couldn't speak.

Marianne whispered, "We'll get through this, we will. I don't even know how, I just know we will."

Squeezing Greenlee's hand she whispered, "Greenlee, *The Greenlee Project* page . . . it's gone now."

After Marianne left, Greenlee sat disconsolately on her bed, her legs drawn up and arms wrapped around her knees. *I'm not like that,* she thought. *I'm not the person they say I am. I know that.* She reflected a while longer. *I know who I am.* Greenlee sat straight up on her bed. *I'm Greenlee Lynn Granger—I know what I have to do.*

Chapter 11 - Can You Hang?

Clay pulled out a seat and sat down. He was starting to settle in, make friends, and get caught up in school, but he still had a problem. His teammates weren't coming around as fast as he'd hoped, and it bothered him. He wasn't used to being so low on the totem pole, especially considering how talented he was. It was usually the other way round; people tried to befriend him. Tucker, a massive linebacker, walked into the classroom and spoke to him. For some reason Tucker liked him.

"Hey dude, 'sup?"

Clay tipped his head and Tucker playfully nudged him as they took their seats. Clay wondered if the dude had any idea how strong he was. Tucker had been showing him around and keeping him in the team loop. He'd told Clay not to worry about A.J., that he had his back if it got out of hand. That was kinda cool; but Clay knew a bond between him and A.J. was doubtful, even if Tucker thought they'd eventually all work it out.

"He'll come around, you'll see. You'll like him," Tucker said. "He's a cool dude."

Clay kept his cool. Everybody loved A.J. and keeping a spot on the team was the only thing on Clay's mind.

Tucker coughed into his hands and made a snide comment about the English teacher. Everyone cracked up and Clay laughed too. This class did suck! Clay's mind was on the girl sitting two rows over and three seats down. She was hot, at least to him. What was her name again? She'd said it enough. He racked his brain, glanced her way from time to time, and then it came to him.

Laurel. That girl's name was Laurel. Unusual name, he thought. He liked unusual. She'd been pretty obvious about trying to get his attention, he'd actually noticed, and he was always oblivious to stuff like that. Girls flirting with him, yep, Clay missed it every time.

Kelsey passed Laurel a note: *Don't look now, but hot new guy is staring at you!* Laurel smiled. She liked that others noticed, especially the girls. Flipping her hair, she dug through her purse and glossed her lips. Shiny and kissable, she faced forward.

"Oh, P u h l e e e e e e z e," mumbled Kelsey, dragging out the word *please*.

Laurel shot her a smirk, "You're just jealous, shut up already."

"True dat!" said Kelsey.

She did wish Clay were looking at her, but they always looked at Laurel. The bell finally rang and everyone piled out of the room as fast as they could; the faster they were out of there, the longer they had to mingle in the halls. Everyone tried to check their phones without getting caught. The teachers turned the other way, tired of being the phone police, and checked their own phones.

Marianne waited at the end of the hall with Audrey; Greenlee walked toward them, checking her phone from the inside of her purse. A group of boys checked her out as she walked by, but she didn't notice, she never did. Marianne and Audrey noticed.

"Not cool!" Greenlee said as she approached. "Really?"

Tucker walked beside Clay, ignoring Laurel. She was clueless. Football, trucks, hunting, hanging out with the boys, and of course parties, these were the things worth talking about. The small talk she was coming up with was boring at best. Tucker took it upon himself to do Clay a favor and save him.

"Golden, it's time," he said, pointing at his watch, and they headed toward the field house.

Clay stayed away from A.J. He did what Coach Davis told him to do, no questions asked, and the boys listened to him without giving him a hard time. They stepped up, covered him, found holes on the field that he hadn't seen and managed to catch the ball almost every time. Practice had gone well and Coach had noticed. Clay was finding his rhythm again and it was starting to show. Coach blew his whistle, went over a few things and dismissed them. A.J. didn't make any comments, and neither did Clay. They walked to the locker room as if the other one did not exist. The tension brewing between the two was obvious, yet never discussed. Clay showered, dressed, and checked his phone: one text from Laurel. It read **hope to see ya later**. He didn't respond, deleted it, and left the locker room.

"Meeting in the parking lot," Tucker snickered. "Team meeting, if you know what I mean?" He winked and left the locker room.

His first official invite to an off-field get-together with the team! Clay was pumped and had every intention of going, regardless of what they were doing. He threw his gear in the back of his truck. Tucker pulled down the tailgate. A few of his teammates sat on the back and made themselves comfortable.

"Ready to hang?" Tucker asked.

Clay smirked. He'd been ready, "Let's go!"

"Good. I think we're going over to Zane's for a bit; his parents won't be back for a while. Oh yeah, can I have a ride?" Tucker asked. Turning to the guys perched on the tailgate he said, "Move it boys, time to go!"

Clay texted his dad: **Text mom for me, will ya? Hanging out with the guys.**

Clay fired up his truck and his teammates were impressed. It was loud, just the way every guy liked it, and even though it wasn't a brand-new truck, it was still cool: cobalt blue four-by-four, complete with lift kit, eight cylinders, and low mileage. His dad had done good!

"Cool truck, man," Tucker said with a sign of approval. "You been mudding in this thing?"

Clay grinned, "Not yet!"

"We'll take it out and break it in, I know a great spot."

Clay couldn't wait. "Excellent."

Several boys had already arrived at Zane's house by the time they pulled up. Cars and trucks were piled in the driveway and the street, but the house seemed unusually quiet for such a crowd. Zane's neighbors apparently took it upon themselves to head up a watchdog group that constantly monitored the noise level and kept watchful for anything out of the ordinary.

Griff answered the door and led them down a long hallway toward the sound of laughter and guys being guys, talking trash and cutting up. The house was big, and Clay knew they were headed to some type of game or media room. He was right. It was a huge game room with a pool table, a dartboard, an old pinball machine up against the wall, and neon signs. *Cool room*, Clay thought as he glanced around trying not to look too obvious that he was impressed.

Josh and Hayden were playing pool and there were other boys scattered around the room, talking and goofing around. Out of the corner of his eye, Clay noticed A.J. sitting on a couch with some guy he didn't recognize. A.J. noticed him too, but didn't acknowledge him and Clay pretended he hadn't noticed the slight. Tucker stood in the middle of the room and proceeded to make an announcement.

"Listen up!" The room went silent. "Golden boy has graced us with his presence." Laughter broke out at Clay's expense. "Let's try to make him feel welcome . . . all right?" Tucker tried to make eye contact with A.J., but A.J. wasn't paying any attention to what Tucker was saying.

The guys continued doing what they were doing. Clay didn't say anything, but he'd have given anything if Tucker had just kept his fat mouth shut!

Zane pointed to a small fridge behind a bar. "Drinks are in there, help yourself."

On the TV there were girls running around in tiny bathing suits playing beach volleyball. Clay took a second to admire a busty girl, who almost lost her top, which only added fuel to the fire as cheers erupted throughout the room.

"Dude she's hot!" Griff pointed to the same girl falling out of her suit. "Gotta love beach volley ball."

By the time the boys were done, chips, pretzels and even cold pizza had landed on the floor. Zane wasn't concerned about the mess and for good reason: standing in the doorway was a massive bulldog.

"Watch," he laughed. "He'll eat anything. He might puke, just saying, but he'll clear this crap up."

Curtis, the fattest English bulldog Clay had ever seen, had already started slobbering. Drool dripped everywhere. Zane wasn't kidding; Curtis ate all of it, gagging only once, after a pretzel went down the wrong way. Griff dropped extra stuff on the floor just to see if Curtis would eat it. Clay observed and couldn't help but think, *Zane's a senior and I'm at his house. This is a good night!*

The nickname *Golden* seemed to have stuck. That sucked, but at least he had a nickname. He was having fun despite his unseen nervousness. He watched as A.J. interacted with all of them with ease, and he felt a surge of jealousy run through him. He wanted to be that kid again, the one that got along with everyone and the one that everyone wanted to know. He continued to listen as the boys talked smack and teased each other, and it didn't take long for the conversation to turn to football. It did, however, take a very weird turn, an unexpected one: initiations. It was the first time A.J. had actually spoken to him, and even Clay knew that most likely it wasn't a good thing.

"Everyone goes through initiation," A.J. smirked. "Do or die, as we say. Right, boys?" and everyone laughed, but Clay noticed that no one disagreed.

One by one they shared bits about their own personal initiations. It didn't sound that bad. Clay laughed, nervously, but as he laughed he wondered, *Seriously, is this a joke?* "That's kinda cool," he said. *This crap's for college, right?* he thought. "Sounds like fun," he said.

Clay noticed that he was the center of attention once again. Tucker patted his back and slammed a soda. "No one knows about this, dude, it's our thing. We're sworn to secrecy."

The thought of an opportunity to prove himself off the field in the eyes of his teammates terrified him and thrilled him. What if his parents found out? What if he let his dad down? Thoughts flashed through his mind faster than he could answer them. He'd worked so hard and finally he had a chance to fit in. Initiation. How bad could it be?

"Hell, I'm in," he stated, staring into the eyes of A.J., his adversary. "Bring it!"

The boys hollered with approval; the new kid might make it after all! Tucker gave him thumbs up; Griff, a knuckle-bump. A.J placed an arm around Clay's shoulder. A.J. laughed. Clay was now sure that this couldn't be a good thing!

Clay's voice wasn't as strong as he'd hoped, but he tried to disguise it. "What do I have to do?" he asked, but as soon as the words left his mouth, an idea popped into his head.

"I have an idea . . . what if I come up with my own initiation?" Clay asked the group.

"That's not really how it works," Tucker replied and Griff agreed.

"Yeah . . . half the fun is making you do stuff."

Surprising Clay, A.J. spoke up. "I don't think we've ever had anyone initiate himself," he said sarcastically, "but there's a first time for everything and that would definitely qualify as one." He nudged Zane, who raised his eyebrows, indicating that he wasn't opposed to it.

"You realize you'd have to come up with something original and out there before we'd even consider it, right? But if you can do that, you're already halfway there, you know what I mean?" A.J. grinned, "Heck, if it's good, we might even use the idea again and name it after you!"

"Nothing cheesy," Griff laughed.

"No, dude. It's gotta be cool and we, as a group, have to approve it before he does it. Agreed?" It took a minute but the yeses came in.

"OK. Clay, you've got one week to decide what your initiation into the brotherhood will be. Got it?"

"Fair enough!" Clay responded, glancing at the boys. "I can do that!"

Chapter 12 - Name It!

It was dark, had been for hours, but Clay couldn't sleep. Tossing and turning, worrying about what he'd gotten himself into, had taken over his mind. Performing an actual task didn't seem as daunting as coming up with an idea that would impress his entire team. Possible scenarios raced through his mind. The problem was that most of them had been done before, and if they hadn't been done, the team had suggested them already. Bragging rights for originality had seemed like a great idea at the time, but certainly not now. Staring out of his window, Clay started to think. For a split second he'd considered pulling his dad aside and discussing his options, but he knew that was crazy! Surely, even though Clay was trying to please him, his dad would disapprove of what he was about to do.

Clay paced the floor, continuing to wrack his brain, but nothing. *Breathe*, he told himself. *Relax*. It will come to you, it always does. He couldn't seem to convince himself, but kept saying it over and over again, as if hoping to make it come true. His last glance at the clock before he finally lay down and dozed off was 4:40 a.m., one hour before his alarm went off. When his alarm went off, he struggled to get out of bed. Splashing cold water on his face helped, but Clay knew he looked as bad as he felt. He was overwhelmed, and when he went downstairs, his mom knew immediately something was amiss.

"Good morning," said Clay.

Placing a bowl of oatmeal down in front of him, she studied his face, staring at him in an odd way. "Are you all right? You look tired."

"Yeah, studied kinda late, that's all," he said. "I'm just tired." That last part was at least true.

She smiled. "Want one?" she offered pouring her self a cup of coffee cup. He shook his head, and she placed the pot back on the burner. *What a great kid she had*, she thought to herself.

Clay tried to unlock his truck but the door wouldn't open. Realizing he'd picked up the wrong set of keys, he turned back toward the house. His mom met him halfway and tossed his set to him.

"Boy, you are tired!"

He smiled half-heartily at her. "Love ya, gotta go."

Usually Clay cranked up his stereo, but he didn't that morning. Arriving at school, he didn't have a clue as to how he'd gotten there. Between worry, lack of sleep, and knowing that A.J. would be waiting for him, he hadn't remembered a single turn, stop sign, or another car on the road.

Clay noticed a girl as he walked across the parking lot. She was being dropped off, right in front of the school steps, and embarrassing exchanges with the parental unit were clearly taking place. She was trying to leave and he could tell that she was uncomfortable because her parent kept talking to her. He stared at her, but because he was tired, he stared too long. He noticed that she didn't seem to notice, which was interesting to him. Every girl noticed when he looked at her, and she wasn't anything spectacular to look at, average at best. He blew it off, having too much on his mind anyway, until he heard her name: Greenlee. Some kid called out from across the parking lot, "Greenlee." He couldn't help but notice that it was a cool name. Greenlee, now that was an unusual name.

As soon as he turned the corner by his locker, he stopped dead in his tracks. Tucker and Griff were waiting for him, snickering among themselves, and he could tell immediately that his locker looked as if someone had puked Pepto Bismol all over it. Pink streamers, balloons, and some girlie unmentionables were plastered from top to bottom. It made Clay grin, but the boys, pleased with themselves, laughed hysterically. Clay started grabbing at the pink crepe paper and let it fall to the floor. He was too tired to be embarrassed and kinda glad that they'd taken the time to kid around with him. Once he got to the granny-sized pink panties, he finally just gave in and cracked up with the other boys.

"Dude, it's a celebration. The big announcement is today, right?" Tucker nudged Griff. "So what are you going to do . . . you know what I mean, right?"

Clay faked a smile. "I'll announce it when the team's all together, no point in explaining it twice, you *know* what I mean?"

"Hope it's good," Griff said as he patted Clay on the back. "If not, it's gonna suck to be you."

He didn't need to be reminded. The bell was about to ring and he couldn't afford to be late; it ticked Coach off when his team was late for class.

"I know A.J.'s dying for me to fail here," Clay said to the guys.

"Ya think? Of course he is." Griff shoved him into a group of girls that were walking toward the science lab. "Heads up ladies, loser coming through." He laughed at his own comment and added, "Seriously dude, of course he wants you to fail, no offense. But it's not personal."

Clay looked at him as if he'd lost his mind.

Griff laughed, "Yeah you're right; what am I thinking? Of course it's personal!"

It was the one reason that Clay didn't want A.J. to pick his task. Assigning the initiation would give A.J. the opportunity to set him up for failure. He didn't want to fail and had never considered himself a failure, but for the first time since he'd arrived, he believed he was about to.

"He feels freaked out right now, you know, about his position on the field. If you fail at your initiation, you lose respect. That for sure will shake you up. He wants that. He doesn't want to share the limelight, and you wouldn't want to, either."

"Stop talking dude—not helping."

Maybe Clay would feel the same way as A.J. did, but he didn't think so.

In class, the teacher was lecturing about simple organisms: bacteria, fungi, and algae. Clay heard the words, but comprehended nothing. Planning his initiation was posing a problem. He was desperate. The hot girl walking between the seats toward the front of the class was a nice distraction. She asked the teacher if she could be excused. Sick, she'd said, not feeling well, but the teacher never looked up.

"You look fine."

"Really," Laurel snapped loud enough for the entire class to hear. "I'm cramping; pretty sure you have no idea what that feels like, right?"

He'd heard it all before, didn't believe her, but didn't want to deal with her. Handing her a yellow hall pass, he continued reading, told her she had five minutes to get to the bathroom, get back, sit down, shut up, and quit disturbing his class.

Laurel waltzed back to her seat, grabbed her purse, and left the room. Clay liked the way she did that, the waltzing out thing, with confidence and he liked it. A lot of attitude for such a cute girl and he thought it was sexy.

Checking each stall, making sure no one intruded, Laurel turned the facet on full blast and let the water run down the sink. She pulled a warm soda out of her purse, slammed it down, and ran into a stall. Bending over the bowl, she barfed with ease. The vomit rushed into her mouth, burning her throat the entire way as it came up. It was disgusting, dangerous, and gross. She wiped her mouth and stared into the bowl, embarrassed and yet relieved at the same time. She pretended it was the last time, but she knew it probably wasn't. If she didn't get a handle on it soon, she promised herself to get some help. She hated herself for being so stupid. She realized it was out of control, and for the first time admitted to herself that she may have a problem.

Stepping out of the stall, she checked the bathroom, rinsed her mouth at the sink, straightened her hair, and left. Furiously she chewed a piece of sugar-free gum and reminded herself that even if she got the help she needed, she still couldn't be fat. She took her seat and noticed Kelsey staring at her. She was shaking her head and Laurel knew that look: Kelsey disapproved. She was damaging her body by being overly obsessed with her weight. Knowing that Laurel was in a scary situation left her in a difficult position. Laurel refused to accept that her friend knew, ignored the nasty look, and sat down.

"*W h a a a t?*" Laurel said defensively, dragging out her syllables. "Why are you staring at me like that?"

Kelsey didn't respond—no point. Laurel ignored her friend in retaliation. Greenlee heard the exchange between the girls and passed a note to Audrey.

Girl drama . . . BP (Beautiful People) lol.

Audrey glanced toward Laurel and was met with a blank stare. Her written response back to Greenlee: *Big drama. BP headed south. So funny! Haha!*

It finally hit him. His idea for his own initiation finally popped into his head. Feverishly Clay scribbled his idea down on a piece of paper so that he wouldn't forget. As the details came to him, he filled them in. It had come to him so weird-like, without thinking really, that he couldn't believe it. It was a lucky break.

Kelsey had been irritated with the hot girl, Laurel, and he'd been distracted by Kelsey. She was staring at him and he caught her, which was funny, because she pretended she wasn't staring when she clearly was. Overcompensating, she did the nervous girl thing. He stared at her, and she started to blush. She was uncomfortable, with cheeks red and flushed. His mind went back to his initiation. He needed time to prepare, time to fine-tune his plan before presenting it to the team. It had to be perfect. Relief suddenly swept over him as his wheels were spinning ninety-to-nothing. Could he do it? *Well of course he could.* How long would he have to do it? *That would depend on the guys.* How long could the team keep it a secret? *The team may put a time limit on it; he hoped so.* He'd actually like to get it over with and get on with football. For the first time since he'd heard the words initiation, Clay could finally relax and breathe.

Later that afternoon, standing in the locker room out of Coach's earshot, the boys circled around Clay. As if in a huddle waiting for a play, A.J. called him on it.

"Name it."

Eagerly they waited to see if Clay would have an epic fail, which most of them had hoped, or would his idea be worth something?

"No worries, I've got it," Clay responded. "It's gonna take a minute to organize but it will be worth the wait, I promise you that. This initiation will go down in history, mark my words, boys, history!" He paused, wondering if his announcement would truly WOW them.

"Dude, spill it already. Details," A.J. said.

"The Greenlee Project."

"The Greenlee what?" everyone asked in unison.

"The Greenlee Project," Clay repeated confidently. "I'm about to pull off the biggest inside joke this school has ever witnessed and the only people privy to it are standing in this room. Greenlee is my project. Some girl named Greenlee, average at best, is about to become a 24/7 live project, without her knowledge of course, thus *The Greenlee Project*."

Dead silence. The boys were speechless. Clay laid out his plan in as much detail as he had so far.

"First things, first," he said. "Set up a private group on the Teen2Teen site and inst-a-post sites. We, the team, will have access. The objective is to turn the girl, Greenlee, into an ongoing 24/7 live project. The level of difficulty will increase with the participation of missions or objectives pledged by you morons."

A.J. interjected. "Players have faked girls out before during initiations with dates, dances, whatever. But an ongoing humiliation trip, with posts and team involvement! Well, even I have to admit this takes the game to a brand-new level." Nodding his head and shoving Clay, he added, "Nice one, dude! I can't wait to see the webpage. Is it just gonna be us involved?" Pausing,

A.J. continued, "Seriously, I think I'm impressed." A.J. laughed and his teammates laughed too.

"Yeah dude, I'm impressed: TGP, *The Greenlee Project*. This is gonna be fun," said Griff.

Grabbing hold of Clay, they hoisted him into the air and passed him around the locker room on their shoulders, chanting over and over, *The Greenlee Project, The Greenlee Project, The Greenlee Project.* Clay hadn't done anything yet and they were already impressed. This was going to be great and getting the actual task started would be a piece of cake!

Chapter 13 – Phase 1

Between football, which he loved, and the acceptance of his initiation suggestion, and getting TGP in motion, Clay was busy. A designated time to set up the site was in place and Tucker would help him. It wasn't that he needed assistance, but Tucker had volunteered and that was a good sign. Clay needed to snag a photo of Greenlee for the site and Tucker had been assigned to design the banner, which would have to be something cool. Clay sent a group message to all the guys.

Clay – **Let the games begin, code name T G P**
A.J. – **'Bout time**
Griff – **Bwhaaaa**

After practice Clay tracked Laurel down. His plan definitely had included her, though indirectly. He wasn't bringing her into the TGP picture, but he liked her, and she evidently liked him. His phone was blowing up; texts were coming in, lots of them from the guys and one from his mom, and a smiley face from Laurel. That one made him smile. Clay grinned.

Tucker – **Got the pic yet?**
Clay – **On it**
Tucker – **Ready when you are**

Laurel was where he thought she'd be—at her locker. Kelsey, Brittany, and a couple of girls were standing around her. No surprise there. The Greenlee girl was nowhere in sight, but he wasn't worried. He had a class with her, so it was no big deal. Laurel was the key girl to getting close to the project; at least Clay thought she was. *Kill two birds with one stone*, he thought, *complete this initiation and get to know Laurel a bit more.* She didn't look surprised to see him as he approached her and he liked that.

"Hey."

She said it first. He liked that, too. He responded back and kept walking. All of a sudden he stopped, turned and asked Laurel a question that took her off guard.

"Do you have the homework from last Thursday, the one about the algae?"

All of the girls stared at Clay. That homework paper was from over a week ago.

"Seriously?" Laurel asked.

"No zeroes per Coach, you know what I mean? I'd rather get a lower grade than a zero. No pass, no . . . "

"Yeah I know, play. We've got it or I should say Kelsey does." Laurel smiled and pointed to Kelsey, who wasn't amused.

"JK," she laughed. "Seriously Kelsey, we did our homework, right?"

"I did my homework," Kelsey said with notable irritation in her voice. "You copied it, so I guess *we* did it," she continued. "Now he'll copy it, so I guess he's done his homework too."

"Well there ya go." Laurel said. "I guess you can thank Kelsey that we've all completed the assignment." She laughed. Clay thought she had a great laugh. "Oh yeah, by the way," she added, "you made an A!"

Kelsey pulled a black plastic binder from her backpack, handed him the report on algae and told him not to plagiarize. "I'll share, but I won't sacrifice my grades, got it? I go down, you go down."

Clay grinned, thanked her, but he had no intention of using it. He'd finished his assignment over a week ago. He just wanted to see how far he could go. Snapping a few pics, he thanked her again and handed back her paper.

"Don't want to lose it, you know what I mean."

"Ah . . . smart guy! Like it," Laurel said sarcastically.

Awkward small talk was all he managed on his way to class. When he finally sat down at his desk, he realized Greenlee wasn't there yet. He scanned the room to make sure he hadn't missed her when he came in, but she wasn't there. Sliding his hand into his pocket he pulled out his phone, pretended to read a text, and waited for her to enter the classroom. She finally walked in with her friends and sat down two rows over and three seats back from Laurel. Quickly he snapped a picture in her direction and took another of Griff, who was sitting on the other side of the class, just to cover his tracks. The teacher glared at him and motioned in his direction, indicating that he should put his phone away. He wasn't sure how good the photo was because he'd snapped it so quickly, but knowing his luck, she wouldn't even be in it. If that was the case, his only other opportunity would be at lunch and he had no idea if they had the same lunch period. As soon as the bell rang, Greenlee packed up her things and was gone. Man, that girl's fast, he thought. He pulled out his phone and checked the pic. As he had feared, it was no good, so lunch it was. He read his texts:

Tucker – **Did you get it?**
Clay – **Bad image. No good**
Tucker – **You've got another shot—try lunch**
Clay – **That's the plan**

Clay scoped out the cafeteria, looking for Greenlee. She was definitely plain, but she had one friend that had reddish brown hair and stood out. If he could spot the redhead, then he could find that girl. Her other friend was kinda cute, but she dressed weird. He kept his eyes open for her as well. Black seemed to be her signature color, though once he'd seen her from head to toe in gray, all gray, weird. She still wasn't bad looking, but what was with the drab colors?

Clay, Tuck, and Griff sat down at a table in the corner. Griff focused on the hot girls or at least the ones he thought were cute. Not a total waste of time; he might even score a few digits.

"Yo bro, look for the redhead," Clay suggested. "She stands out more than the other one."

Tuck pointed to a small group of girls standing in the *a la carte* line. "Is that them?"

"No. It's one of her friends, though; I've seen her with TGP as well as the redhead," Clay said.

The guys followed the girls as they left the cafeteria and went out and sat in the courtyard. There she was, TGP, sitting at a table under a tree with, lo and behold, the redhead.

"Score," said Clay.

"She's got to be the one in the middle," Tuck whispered. "TGP?"

"Yep, that's her. I'll snap it."

It had been too easy; nobody cared what they were doing. Greenlee, Marianne, and Audrey were all doing the normal girl thing: checking their phones, talking, and picking at their food. Clay snapped the photo he needed and they all left.

Clay texted a message to the group: **Got it.**

"We'll finish setting up the site up after practice, sound good?"

Tuck nodded in agreement. "I'll be there. I've got the banner already picked out. A beautiful kick-butt Polaris ATV. Dude, I so want one," he laughed. "I wish my dad would buy that sucker for real." Tucker's pick was awesome! A black, wicked, four-by-four EPS–Grizzly, 700 F1 special-edition ATV. It was parked on top of a massive mountain that overlooked a rugged range. *Perfect for hunting,* was the subliminal message.

Clay liked four-wheeling and hunting too, and it was a cool banner, plus it wouldn't draw attention to the group, *code name TGP: The Greenlee Project.*

The page was set up as a private group, which included every kid on the team, but only players, no trainers. The password was tgp23raiders, which was sent via group text message immediately. Clay did the honors and posted the photo of Greenlee sitting in the courtyard with her friends. His caption followed.

Clay – **The Greenlee Project— let the games begin!**
Tucker – **Seriously, I think by the end of the week you should be walking her to class. HAHAHAHA!!!**
Griff – **Yeah. Take embarrassing pics & post**
Wesley – **Golden's girl hahahaha!**
Rich – **R we insta-posting yet?**
A.J. – **No dude, 2 soon**
Clay – **Dude that's crazy, insta-post, red flags?**
Danny – **insta-post will b fine, may b later?**
Riley – **Game on Golden, if you got any, lol**
A.J. – **Agreed on insta-post, wait, for now. Yes on walk her butt to class, post pics by wed**
A.J. – **Note that as first official challenge**
Tucker – **Challenge posted. bwaaaaa**

The boys got into the game quickly, caught up in the excitement of knowing they were the only ones who knew what was going on. Others posting challenges took the pressure off Clay, and helped ease the pressure on the field as well. Clay noticed it almost immediately. His plan was in motion, the team was participating, he was playing football, and life was good!

Chapter 14 - Girls Will Be Girls

"I've got nothing to wear!" Greenlee said to her mom.

Here we go again, thought Mrs. Granger. She put the clean laundry on Greenlee's bed, pointed to the pile, and said, "Put those away." She gave her daughter's room the once-over, rolled her eyes, rubbed her temples, left and shut the door. Sometimes shutting the door was the best way to deal with a teen's room. Besides, she wasn't about to have the clothes argument again.

Greenlee flopped down on her bed. Frustrated and sick of fighting with her closet's lack of style she gave up and picked up her phone. Why couldn't she throw a cute outfit together every day like everyone else?

> Greenlee – **What are you wearing tomorrow?**
> Marianne – **Dunno, usual I guess. U?**
> Greenlee – **I have no idea!*@#!**
> Greenlee – **Did u do hmwrk?**
> Marianne – **Nah. U**
> Greenlee – **Nt. Yt. Bt. Fixng 2**
> Marianne – **Cpy Audrey's?**
> Greenlee – **Truth!**
> Greenlee – **I'll text her**
> Marianne – **K CU**
> Greenlee – **TTYL**

At least her math homework would be covered. If Audrey hadn't done it already, she would have completed it by the time it was due and Greenlee would do the next assignment. They had a buddy system that worked, and as long as they didn't get busted, it was all good. She got back to the painful process of deciding what to wear to school for the following day. Sticking her arm into the closet, Greenlee closed her eyes, ran her fingers over the top of the hangers and decided that whatever she pulled out would be what she'd wear. Her closet was a fake antique, handed down from her Aunt Sally. She pulled out a t-shirt and held it up against her chest. With the exception of being a different color, it was the same as the one she'd worn today. Tired of messing with it, she settled on the shirt. Who was she kidding? She couldn't keep up with the *BP* anyway. They made it look easy, but she knew from experience it wasn't. All of them had different outfits every day of the week, they planned to look alike, and of course they always looked amazing. Even on dress-down casual days they looked freaking amazing. They sucked! Feeling sorry for herself, Greenlee muttered under her breath that it didn't matter what she'd look like anyway, because nobody would notice her.

"Why should I even care? Seriously, it's just ridiculous."

With that, she turned off her light and called it a night. She was tired anyway.

The following morning Greenlee overslept. She shoved a bite of toast into her mouth and yelled bye to her mom as she ran out the door. Her dad was frustrated with waiting for her and honked the horn for the second time. He was running late and his daughter's lack of consideration for his schedule was irritating him. Horrified that the neighbors knew he was waiting for her, Greenlee raised her hands in disgust, rolled her eyes, got in the front seat, and slammed the door.

"Seriously!" Greenlee said to her dad.

Mr. Granger tapped his watch. "We're late, and now I'm late. You're making me late."

Greenlee opened the mirror and glossed her lips. "Oh my God, was that really necessary? You totally embarrassed me!"

He didn't answer, but shot a look in her direction that indicated now was a good time for her to stop talking. She could tell he wasn't in the mood; in fact, *ticked* came to mind, although that wasn't the word she was really thinking. She quit talking. Sullen, Greenlee pulled out her phone and texted Marianne the rest of the way to school. They drove in silence as her fingers tapped as fast as they could. Her dad didn't even attempt to make any conversation; he must have been really ticked, she thought, since usually he insisted on small talk during their drive. Greenlee couldn't wait to get out of the car and hit send for her last text as she climbed out.

Greenlee – **Here**
Marianne – **K**

Mr. Granger started to say goodbye, but while he was still in mid-sentence Greenlee slammed the door. He shook his head as he drove off. Guilt immediately swept over her and now her fingers once again tapped the screen on her phone.

Greenlee – **Sorry. Luv ya. I won't be late tomorrow.** ☺

She knew that he wouldn't see her message until after he got to work, but she felt better knowing that he would. She just hoped that he would check his phone soon. It was, after all, her fault in the first place, and he didn't have to drive her. He could make her ride the bus and that would be awful! Marianne struggled to keep up with her as Greenlee stormed toward the concrete steps.

"Slow down!" Marianne pleaded, falling behind. "Greenlee, wait up, seriously."

"I feel like crap for being mean to my dad," Greenlee mumbled under her breath. "I'm sorry, it's not you, but seriously, he shouldn't have honked the horn, right?"

Greenlee pulled a licorice stick out of her bag and stuck it in her mouth. She offered Marianne one. Shocked didn't begin to describe how the girls felt when Laurel walked right up to them, stuck her hand into the candy bag, and pulled out a couple of pieces.

"You don't care, do you?" Laurel asked. "Love these things."

"Help yourself," Greenlee replied, trying to hide her astonishment. "Yeah, me too . . . love these." She acted as normal as possible, but this was weird.

"We're going be late, we better go," Marianne said, shutting her locker and turning to leave. "Let's go," she repeated, as if they needed a signal.

"Yeah, we better go, too," Laurel replied. "See ya later."

"Weird, right?" Marianne asked.

"Yeah . . . the whole thing!"

Clay grinned. He was impressed. Laurel had game! She'd made contact with TGP. The play was in motion.

"Too easy," Laurel whispered in Clay's ear. "Next!"

"I see you met Clay's new friend, Laurel," said Tucker with a smirk. Everyone except for Laurel laughed.

"Whatever!" Laurel snapped back. "Why do you want me to be nice to her anyway?" She took a step back from Clay and looked into his big brown eyes. "What's in it for me?"

"Why, are you jealous?"

Wrong thing to say, but the boys enjoyed it. Laughter broke out. Clay realized that the look on Laurel's face and the fact that her mouth was about to spout something unpleasant in his direction indicated he'd better defuse the situation and fast. He raised his hands and put them on her shoulders.

"As if, it's a joke!" he said. Although his hands felt good on her shoulders, Laurel still wasn't sure what was going on.

"Just kidding about the jealousy thing," said Clay. "That girl thing, the other girl, it's all in good fun."

He winked at her and something about the way he did it made her smile. It was cheesy and stupid, but it gave her a feeling that there was more to come. She had no idea what that could be or if she was reading too much into the way he was looking at her, but she liked it anyway.

"OK. I'll play your game for now, till I figure it out, that is," she said, flipping her hair over her shoulders with her free hand. "Or until I get bored, and then I'm out." She winked at him, turned on her heels, and joined her friends.

In class, Greenlee, Marianne, and Audrey were already seated. Marianne sat and watched everybody enter the room.

"I don't like her," Marianne whispered in Greenlee's ear when Laurel sat down. "My name is Laurel and I'm a stuck up, fake little . . . " she started giggling, no need to finish the sentence.

Greenlee smiled, but didn't comment. Laurel was watching the girls without it being too obvious that she was staring at them. It wasn't easy. She felt like a freaky stalker.

Clay slipped his phone out of his pocket and worked it from his lap. Logging into the site T G P, he made a quick post.

Clay – **Phase 1 in motion**
Tucker – **U sucked**
Clay – **Work in progress lol**
Tucker – **No, u sucked hahaha**
Clay – **Will nail it**
Daniel – **Nail it?**
Clay – **Stop it!!! Hahaha**
Griff – **Golden, u do suck bwaaah**
A.J. – **task already**
Clay – **On it**
Tucker – **r u? On it hahahha**
Clay – **haha, jk, ur NOT funny**
Tucker – **I am funny - hahahahhahahah**
Griff – **(snap & post) Greenlee at locker with Laurel**
Griff – **other girl hot, yes?**
A.J. – **yes . . . very hot**
A.J – **Golden, not u**
Tucker – **hahaha other girl too hot for Golden**
Clay – **Hell no she's not, she likes me**
Wesley – **Dreaming haha**
Clay – **Watch me, hot girl, not other** ☺

Laurel noticed two things during class: (1) Clay kept staring at the plain girl, Greenlee, and (2) Greenlee was oblivious to his stares. That was just weird! A good-looking athlete like Clay, interested in some girl that no one knew or cared about, instead of her, was ridiculous. But he was interested in her; at least he'd indicated that or something. She hadn't imagined it. Laurel scribbled a note and passed it to Brittany.

Who is that girl?

Brittany read it, looked at Laurel, who motioned with her eyes toward Greenlee and mouthed the words, "That one?"

Brittany casually glanced over her shoulder, took a peek at Greenlee, who was way too interested in what the teacher was discussing, shrugged, and turned back around. She didn't know that girl. She passed the note to Kelsey, but her response was the same; she didn't know Greenlee either.

As soon as the bell rang, several kids scrambled toward the door. Running out of time, the teacher hadn't quite finished the point that he'd been trying to make.

"It's like you guys can't wait to leave," he said aloud.

The remaining stragglers felt obliged to laugh, though he knew they were faking it. Clay grabbed Tuck's arm, walking slower, and he gestured to Greenlee. It was time to talk to the girl. Griff hung back to observe, though he wouldn't deny that he would've hit *record* on his phone if given the opportunity. Clay's attempt to pick up the girl, an epic fail for sure, would be Griff's first official post. Greenlee and her friends finally exited the room, but why it had taken them so long, he didn't have a clue. Tucker shoved Clay toward Greenlee but Marianne spun around, taking them all by surprise. Laurel's curiosity had gotten the better of her. She stood across the hall and watched Clay as he approached Greenlee. She waited for their exchange. Laurel wasn't sure if she had an interest in Clay or not, but if she did, she'd make sure he knew it. She couldn't stand it. Insisting her friends stand by, she walked directly toward the boys.

"Clay and your two losers, I guess?" she pointed at Tuck and Griff.

"Wanna check out that new taco place on the corner?" Laurel smiled sweetly at Clay and he immediately nodded.

"Absolutely."

"Great. You drive."

"K," Clay replied coyly, but then to her dismay he turned toward Greenlee. "Wanna go? They can come too, right?" he asked.

Laurel was taken by surprise. "Really? I didn't ask them. I asked you and your loser friends. No offense, but I don't really know them."

"Are you getting this?" Tuck whispered and Griff mouthed yes.

"It's not a big deal," Clay said "It's just, that way we can all get to know each other. I'm driving and I don't care if they go, do you?" He shoved Tucker. "The more the merrier as this idiot would say." Tucker waved, though he was oblivious to what was going on.

"I'm kinda new here, just trying to get to know everybody, you know what I mean?" He winked at Laurel, but she missed his signal.

"Well I don't know her at all, really, but okay. Like I said, no offense," Laurel glanced quickly in Greenlee's direction.

"None taken," Greenlee replied softly.

"I don't know her either," Clay said, "but I don't know a lot of people. So, perfect." He did it again. He winked at her. WTH?

Tucker and Griff burst out laughing. Laurel's face had an odd, slightly red, scrunched-up look and Griff caught it all on camera. Greenlee started to feel incredibly uncomfortable.

"You know, I'm not really hungry. We don't have to go," said Greenlee.

"Don't be silly. Greenlee, isn't it?" Laurel asked. "Of course we'll all go. Like he said, it's a chance to get to know each other."

Clay smiled at Laurel. "You can sit next to me if you want." He nudged her playfully. "Why are you being so mean to your friend?" pointing at Greenlee with a grin. "Just kidding," he whispered.

"Let's just go already," Tucker said. "Now I'm starving."

Marianne couldn't take her eyes off Tucker. That dude was huge and weird. Greenlee was nervous, but observed everyone on the way to the restaurant. Clay kept finding ways to playfully touch Laurel, which made her happy, but she was totally confused.

"Greenlee," Clay startled her when he said her name. "I'm assuming that you guys like tacos?"

"Yep, tacos are good," Greenlee replied.

"Good. This will be fun!"

Greenlee glanced at her friends. Fun? Maybe if the viper, Laurel, behaved herself. She was glad they were going, but she wasn't a hundred percent comfortable, that was for sure.

Chapter 15 – Golden's Moving

Walking to the parking lot was awkward and conversation was at a minimum. Greenlee was nervous but she kept telling herself to relax. *It was just a group of kids eating lunch*, she'd said, *no big deal*, but she *was* glad that Clay had made a big deal out of asking her and not particularly the others. Marianne liked anything that upset the BP and she didn't care what it was. This happened to be perfect because it irritated Laurel and included food. Greenlee had a front-row seat to watch Laurel fume. Greenlee applied lip gloss, which allowed her to hide what she was about to say.

"Is this weird or what?" Greenlee asked Marianne.

"Right." Marianne stared at the odd combination of kids gathered at the truck waiting to go to lunch.

Laurel whispered something obnoxious to her friends. They laughed, but no one cared enough to ask what the comment was.

"Let's go, slowpokes," Laurel yelled as she climbed into the truck. "We've been waiting for you."

"Well, we're here," Marianne yelled back. "Let's go."

Clay turned up his music, rolled down the windows, and took off down the back road behind the high school. The taco place was crowded but they found a booth, squeezed in, and crammed down their food as fast as they could. As far as the tacos went: not bad for ninety-nine cents each. Everything tasted better when it fit your budget.

"Did you hear we have a team meeting after practice tonight?" Clay said with a mouthful of taco.

"Dude, for real?" Tucker knew they had practice, but he'd missed the meeting afterward part.

"Yep. You need a ride home?"

"Yeah bro. Actually I do, thanks."

Tucker took a bite of his taco and in between chews said, "Man, I need a truck!"

"I'll sell ya mine," Griff said. "I want a new one."

"You're selling yours?" it sounded as if Tuck said, but it was hard to tell with so much food in his mouth. "No dude, I don't want yours, but thanks. Seriously, are you selling it for real?"

Griff nodded, "If I can." He grinned. "Hey wait a minute, something wrong with my truck?"

"Nah dude. I just want a brand-new truck, that's all. There's nothing wrong with your truck," Tuck replied.

Griff laughed. "Just kidding, dude. I hate it! I intend to sell that piece of crap just as soon as I have a buyer!"

Everyone thought that was funny and even the BP laughed. A quick check of their phones told them that it was time to go. The girls got up and walked away from the table without picking up their trash.

"Seriously," Tucker screeched. "You girls raised in a barn?"

Greenlee, embarrassed, turned around and walked back toward the table. She had no idea why she hadn't cleaned up her trash. Nerves, maybe? Marianne smirked, rolled her eyes, and made a tacky comment about Tucker being on table duty. His retaliation was to add another comment about her lack of manners and as soon as the words left his mouth, he wished they hadn't.

"Ok . . . take away my man card on that one . . . right!"

"Dude . . . seriously!" Clay shoved him toward the door. "Man, you gotta quit hanging with your mom and sister . . . ugh!"

"I deserved that! Let's go, boys and pigs!"

"You're welcome!" Marianne stated after she'd cleared the table, including Laurel's trash.

"Yeah, thanks," Laurel laughed. "Kelsey was about to get that."

Kelsey rolled her eyes.

"Yeahhh, okay," Marianne said sarcastically, but Greenlee grabbed her arm and changed the subject.

"We need to hurry; we're going to be late," said Griff.

Tucker opened the door to the truck and before anyone else had a chance, Laurel hopped into the front and sat next to Clay. Her face lit up, beaming as if she'd won the prize for the second time that day. Nobody cared or even seemed to notice. The boys were talking football, and Greenlee and her friends were talking about the weekend. It suddenly occurred to Clay that he had a small window of opportunity to make a move on Greenlee for the project and it was narrowing as they approached the school. His mind drifted from practice and back to his initiation. Greenlee's name was on the tip of his tongue, but he couldn't quite pull it off yet.

"Hey . . . what class have you got next?" Clay asked.

The truck got dead quiet.

"Who ya talking to, dude?" Griff's voice suddenly whittled off to a whisper as it occurred to him that Clay was making a move. He slid his hand into his pocket and pushed the record function on his phone.

Clay asked the question again; only this time he had the courage to personalize it. "Greenlee, what class do you have next?"

"Me?" replied a startled Greenlee. There was absolute silence in the truck.

"English," she said hesitantly. "It sucks, right?"

He forced a chuckle. Greenlee asked herself if guys still chuckled?

"Yeah, it does," Clay responded, and she realized that he meant that English wasn't all that great for him either.

Glancing in his rearview mirror, he noticed that she was looking at him. She had pretty eyes—brown, at least they looked brown—but when they accidentally made eye contact, he immediately averted his back to the road. He'd started a conversation but could he keep it going?

"Is that anywhere near D Hall?" he asked.

She nodded. The heat pulsating into her cheeks, the burning indicated that she was blushing. She hated doing that and tried to act as though she wasn't, which always seemed to make it worse. Feeling awkward and out of place, Greenlee stared at her hands, which she placed in her lap. Marianne nudged her in the ribs and smiled. A comforting smile from her friend; just what she needed. Marianne rolled her eyes, made a goofy face, and pointed toward Clay. Clay wasn't done with Greenlee yet. He was just getting started.

"Cool. My class this afternoon is in D. You'll show me where it is, right?"

It wasn't a real question and Greenlee knew it. He'd been to D enough times; they'd seen him in class. Marianne raised her eyebrows and nudged Greenlee's side. Didn't know where it was, yeah right! He was up to something. OMG . . . was he flirting with her? One look between Marianne and Audrey, and yes, he was flirting with her big time.

"It's a big school, dude," Tucker interjected, trying his hardest to act as if he meant it. "I'd take you myself, but I'm on the other side and so is he." He pointed at Griff.

Griff did the one-bob head nod. Pointing to Greenlee he said, "Guess you'll have to show him then."

Greenlee was speechless and Laurel was livid. Marianne was in shock. The guys sat there straight-faced, trying not to laugh, and Griff captured everything on his phone. As soon as Clay parked his truck, Laurel jumped out without saying a word and stormed off. Her friends followed suit. Clay knuckle-bumped the guys, told them that he'd see them later, and turned toward Greenlee.

"Ready?" he asked. "Do you have what you need or do you need to go by your locker?"

Marianne stood at her friend's side, dumbfounded. This dude moved fast! Greenlee grabbed Marianne's sleeve, ensuring that she'd tag along with them.

"I've got everything," said Greenlee.

Griff recorded the departure scene. Clay making hand gestures toward the guys as he and Greenlee walked toward campus. Tucker practically rolling on the floor, already logged into the site, snapped a shot of the two and made a quick post:

Tucker – **Stay posted for more of Golden's smooth moves**

From the school parking lot the boys posted a portion of the conversation between Greenlee and Clay. It was short and lame, but the video of Clay putting on quite the show as he'd managed to glance back at the camera, make obscene gestures toward Greenlee's butt without her knowledge, and maintain a conversation. It was hilarious! Clay did not disappoint. She didn't have a clue. The look on his face indicated he was listening to her, but he hadn't heard a word. Tucker and Griff captured, posted, and made nasty comments about the entire thing. Other comments rolled in as fast as they had posted the initial ones. More of the guys were getting into it. The team was participating. First, second, and third-string names were popping up.

A.J. – **Hahah . . . so freaking funny**

Daniel – **Golden's moving**

Lance – **Walked her to class and then some**

Clay – **Ugh . . . NO! Not the then some . . .**

Tucker – **Yah right**

Griff – **lol**

Dakota – **Dude that's hilarious**

Riley – **Where's the hot girl?**

R.J. – **Other girl/hot**

Clay – **dude, focus TGP**

A.J. – **hahaha . . . add 2 task list?**

Tucker – **May b**

Griff – **IDK 2funny**

A.J. – **BRB**

Clay – **GTG**

Chapter 16 – OMG!

Laurel burst through the stall door, leaned over the toilet bowl, and puked, ridding her body of those nasty tacos she'd choked down, hoping to impress some dude that didn't even notice her. And the thought of being passed over for *Miss Nada* . . . *What the hell!!!* Laurel was out of control and puked again. It made her sick. *Seriously!* Gasping for air, trying to calm herself, she pretended that puking during the middle of the afternoon was totally normal. She knew it wasn't. *I have a serious problem. I think I'm in trouble.* She knew she was in trouble. She promised herself she'd talk to her mom. She needed help.

Kelsey stared at Brittany in horror; Brittany covered her mouth for fear of puking as well. Both girls looked at each other in shock. It was the first time that they'd actually witnessed Laurel puking at will.

"Are you o—" asked Kelsey as Laurel cut her off.

"Don't speak to me right now. In fact, please just shut up!"

"She's just worried about you; so am I," Brittany snapped back in Kelsey's defense. "We're not the enemy here; we're trying to help. We're worried about you!"

"I don't need help!" She wiped her mouth. "I didn't mean that. I do need help and I will talk to my mom."

Laurel pushed past them, walked over to the sink, and rinsed out her mouth with lukewarm tap water.

"I need you to let me handle it. I'll take care of this." She half smiled at them. "OK," they said in unison.

"But we're trusting that you will," added Kelsey.

Embarrassed about Clay, Laurel came up with a defense. "I really didn't like that crap food, though, and that is what all this nonsense is all about!"

Grabbing her purse out of Brittany's hand, for the second time that day she left them standing speechless as she stormed off.

"Do you think she'll tell her mom?" asked Kelsey.

"Oh yeah she will, because if she doesn't, we will!"

Kelsey agreed, "But what do we do for now?"

Brittany hesitated before she spoke, "We watch her. If she's not getting better then we'll intervene. Agreed?"

"Agreed!"

The girls were surprised to find that Laurel was waiting for them halfway down the hall.

"I'll get help," she said. "Seriously though, those tacos were gross, that's all. Nasty comes to mind. They upset my stomach as soon as I ate them." She ran her fingers nervously through her hair and pulled it up high on top of her head, acting as if she wasn't quite sure what to do with it, but settling on a ponytail. "I need some air," she said softly. "I wish that we weren't cutting it this close to class."

"They were kinda greasy," Kelsey added, not knowing what else to say. Trying to ease the tension, she changed the subject but she wished she'd kept her mouth shut.

"Hey, did you guys catch Clay flirting with that girl?"

"OMG . . . Seriously, Kelsey, just shut up already!"

"What? Laurel, what did I say now?"

"OMG . . . let's just go already. I'm so done here!"

In class, Greenlee was on cloud nine. Clay had asked her and her friends to lunch, although Laurel had tagged along, and had then walked her to class. What was with that? He was cute! She tried to remember each detail the best she could, from climbing into his truck, to the amount of tacos he ate, the drive back to school and, last but not least, his walking with her to class. Clay Monning would definitely be the topic of conversation as soon as the girls could talk. Not a bad topic, Greenlee thought, trying to hide her smile. But she couldn't help it: she was too happy.

Laurel, Brittany, and Kelsey were all late for class. The bell rang and apparently none of them had been by the office since they didn't have tardy passes in their hands. Especially irritating was the fact that the girls acted as if the teacher shouldn't care that they were late. They were there now, that should be enough, right?

"Ladies, glad you could finally join us. Hope it wasn't too much trouble!" said the teacher.

The sarcasm that rolled off her tongue with ease was perfectly clear: being late to her class was unacceptable.

"Sorry we're late, we had a . . . " was cut short with a mere wave of the teacher's hand. She didn't accept excuses and she certainly didn't want them, but she had something to say.

"If you don't care about your education at your age, then there's not a lot left that I can say or do for you." She looked them up and down and rolled her eyes. "Sit down!"

"Ewww."

"Booya."

"Dang."

"Akward."

"Bam!"

The comments from the rest of the class kept coming but the teacher didn't stop them. A little peer humiliation would serve them right. She couldn't legally insult them the way she'd like to, but that was the next best thing. They were spoiled brats.

"Get to class on time! No excuses."

Audrey scribbled a note, passed it to Greenlee. It was about the hot guy's cute friend, and how they'd ticked off the BP by being invited to lunch in the first place. Leaving campus, way cool, and oh yeah, did she like that dude, Clay? Any one of those things made for a great conversation during class, but put the three things together, and it was a massive afternoon convo for the girls! Notes flew back and forth. They could hardly keep up without getting caught, but they did a pretty good job trying.

Audrey: *OMG! We ticked off Laurel. How freaking funny is that?*

Marianne: *T.B.H. If we could do that every day it wouldn't hurt my feelings!*

Greenlee: *It was funny. Did you see her face when he walked down D with us?*

Audrey: *His friend is cute. Tucker.*

Marianne: *Other one, loser. Capital L*

A kick to the back of her chair with such force that it not only startled Greenlee, but disturbed the entire class, jolted her chair forwarded and made a God-awful screeching noise as it scraped across the floor.

"WTH!" said Greenlee.

Everyone turned around and stared at her, including Laurel. Greenlee, for the second time that afternoon, turned bright red. Marianne glared at Clay. He stared at Greenlee and mouthed the word, "S O R R Y."

He wasn't sure if she believed him, but he tapped her shoulder and whispered. "Sorry, didn't mean to kick it."

Greenlee bobbed her head, acknowledging his apology, but still trying to get rid of the redness in her face. She looked down at her paper, focusing on anything other than her burning cheeks. Griff was acting like an idiot, messing with his phone and chuckling. He was sent out of the room, but unlike Greenlee, he took it all in stride. Gathering his things, amid stares and smart comments, he raised both of his arms in the air and walked to the front of the room. He grabbed the piece of paper that the teacher held in front of her outstretched hand, turned, faced the class, and smarted off.

"My hall pass?"

"It's your invitation to visit the principal," she countered.

Unconcerned, Griff exited the room.

"All right, time to get back to work people, now pay attention."

Tucker handed Clay his phone. The post that Griff managed to make before being kicked out of class was hilarious. He'd captured Greenlee jolting forwarded and turning beet red. Though the force of the kick had been by accident, the timing was amazing. He'd captured her humiliation, posted it, and the comments appeared immediately. Tucker placed his hand over his mouth, trying not to laugh as he and Clay read the posts. Additional comments kept piling in. They were posting fast. Some of the users they didn't recognize.

"Dude, who is that—Duckdog?" Clay asked.

Tucker shook his head. "Man, I don't know, but funny post, and cool user name!"

Clay – **Next???**
A.J. – **Date night Golden boy**
Tucker – **HaHaHa**
Griff – **Priceless Golden, kicked across the floor**
Clay – **Right, did you see it. Lol . . . course you did**
Griff – **Yah . . . everyone did**
A.J. – **Post a task**
Clay – **Bring it**
Duckdog **– Pics**
Clay – **Who is this?**
Duckdog – **Pics**
Duckdog – **Dude that was funny—her face, red**

The teacher stood by Clay and Tucker. "Phones, now! I'm done! It's a $20.00 fine to get them back and payable to the office."

The bell rang and students poured out of class, except for Tucker and Clay. Begging for another chance, promising never to pull out their phones again, they tried to get them back. Against her better judgment, the teacher reluctantly handed over their phones.

"Don't ever let me see those back in my class again," she warned. "I will not be half as kind if there's another incident." She peered at each one of them. "Are we clear?"

Simultaneously they answered, "Yes ma'am."

"Get out of here before I change my mind!"

As soon as their phones were in their hands, they checked the posts; they were coming in left and right. Some were hilarious and some even offered suggestions for the next phase.

> Justin – **hahaha thought G girl down w the foot, back of the chair, dude**
> Clay – **Man, seriously, didn't expect that**
> Justin – **funny**
> Griff – **Dead RED**
> Clay – **wuz funny**
> A.J. – **like**
> Tucker – **hahaha**
> Ryan – **Next**
> Duckdog – **Cheering section, next game**

Upon hitting the locker room, Clay scrambled to get changed and wondered if Greenlee had thought that he'd really meant to kick the back of her seat that hard. He kinda felt bad about that, but not the posts, because she didn't know about those. But he really hadn't meant to kick her that hard. The guys seemed to think he'd done it on purpose and he said nothing to the contrary. They'd thought it was funny, and the rest was history.

Coach's game plan seemed to be beat the crud out of the whole team on the field in preparation for the game on Friday night. Walkersville Badgers: that didn't sound too fierce, but the Raiders knew better than to underestimate the team. They'd been beat by them before and even though they'd won against them, they almost hadn't. It had been a hard win, but they'd all played a respectable game.

"Get your butts out there on the field. Stretch and get ready, now!" Coach Davis' face was flushed and by the look of it, his assistants had just been put through the ringer. Friday night's game had him stressed and he didn't intend to stress by himself.

"I believe I said now and that means NOW!"

Everyone felt the wrath of Coach at practice. "Do it again. Do it again!" seemed to be all they heard from Coach that afternoon.

"Golden, seriously, do it again and this time do it right!" he called out as he blew his whistle. "A.J., get in there and tell that boy to step down!"

Clay looked across the field, not knowing what he'd done wrong. He raised his hands and yet he knew better than to say a word. Putting them down again, he walked toward the sidelines.

"A.J., do it like I told you!" Coach hollered. "Do it the way we discussed watching the film."

Clay stood by Coach and watched as Coach continued to yell at his team from the sidelines. A.J. did what he was told to do and he did it perfectly. Clay was supportive and rallied around A.J. when the boys came in.

"Nice one!"

"Thanks dude!"

"Hit the showers. I think you guys should've worked ten times harder than that, but you can make it up to me in the morning."

Chapter 17 - Let's Talk

Greenlee had decided that the chair incident had been an accident after all, a fluke. She had captured Clay's expression in her mind's eye at the exact time he'd mouthed the word *Sorry,* and to her he'd seemed sincere. His dark eyes, suddenly massive, complete with raised eyebrows, appeared genuinely startled by the actual force of the kick he'd delivered to the back of her chair. Maybe he didn't realize how strong he was? *He'd said sorry,* Greenlee convinced herself that the embarrassing occurrence hadn't been a big deal after all. *OMG . . . he asked us, me, to lunch!* And there she was . . . back to being a giddy teenage girl, thrilled that the hot new guy had paid attention to her. She couldn't wait to rehash every detail of every word that had transpired with Clay with her friends.

Running into the kitchen she grabbed a bag of chips, a soda, and a piece of fruit, so her mom wouldn't yell at her for her terrible eating habits. She managed a casual response to her mom regarding her day, but that was about it. She took off toward her bedroom. Her mom asked if she was okay, which puzzled Greenlee, who responded that she was fine and continued up the stairs. Slipping off her jeans and throwing on a pair of shorts, she made herself comfortable. Two seconds later, she logged into the Teens2Teens site. Scrolling down the posts she added a few comments, hit a couple of likes and even shared a few posts. Though instant messaging was the rage, Teens2Teens was still a popular site. Just as she was about to log off, Clay Monning popped back into her head. She stared at the top right-hand corner of the page and there was the search box. Hesitating, she typed one letter at a time: C-l-a-y M-o-n-n-i-n-g. She could hear his voice in her head and visualize his smile. She could even picture his walk. It was so weird! Her heart racing, palms sweaty, she finally hit *enter. So messed up,* she thought. *What am I doing? OMG I'm a stalker!!!* Taking a deep breath and exhaling, she continued to sit and stare at his name. *So stupid!* She'd never acted this way before; in fact, they laughed at girls that acted this weird. Several possible matches appeared, yet his profile picture immediately stood out. She wasn't about to message or friend him, but she did stare at his photo. He was so cute. She couldn't believe how cute he looked, even in his profile picture. Just as cute as he did in person; man, she hated that! She jumped out of her skin when her mother came up behind her, peered over her shoulder and spoke.

"Do you have homework, young lady?"

"OMG, you scared me. I already did it."

"Already?"

"Yep, did it in class, in fact, before fifth period."

"Mmm, actually that doesn't surprise me. Good girl!" Greenlee's mother continued. "Put away your clothes and bring me your whites, and grab your dirty towels while you're at it. Got it?"

No answer. Her mom stopped and waited. There was still no response.

"Excuse me. Hello?"

"Sorry! Marianne's coming over, is that okay?"

Her mother's response was the usual. "That's fine if her parents say it's okay. Any questions regarding your laundry?"

"Audrey may come too."

"Again fine, but any questions regarding your chore?"

"I'm on it!"

A.J. group-messaged the team. It was time for Golden to step it up and it was time for everyone to start posting suggestions for Phase 2. They could start posting that evening on *The Greenlee*

Project Page (TGP) between eight and nine. Clay liked that idea. It took the burden off him, having everyone contribute.

> Tucker – **We can post B4 then, right?**
> A.J. – **Right**
> Griff – **I've got one**
> Clay – **Post it**
> Griff – **Will do. BTW it rocks!**

Hearing the doorbell ring, Mrs. Granger opened the door and pointed up the stairs. "She's in her room, go on up." Almost like an afterthought she added, "Would you girls like a soda or something?"

They politely declined and ran up the stairs, shoving each other playfully and bumping into the walls before finally bursting into Greenlee's room. They were laughing so hard by the time they hit the door that Greenlee had to laugh as well.

"Wow, you guys are quiet!" She giggled. "Hey, look at this I pulled up. It's Clay's profile pic on the Teen2Teens site. He's cute, right?"

They agreed that he was cute, and Greenlee couldn't help but lose herself in his crooked grin. Audrey plopped down on the floor in front of the bed and reached for the laptop.

"Can I see that a second?" she asked. "Do you think the other guy is cute too, his friend that's always with him? What's his name? Tucker?"

"Tucker something . . . what was it?" Marianne asked.

"Good question. What is that guy's last name? Mental note to self," Audrey stated out loud. "Find out."

Greenlee plugged Clay's name in again and continued to stare at his profile pic. He was in his football uniform. He had a cute crooked grin on his face, and looked confident in his own skin. Greenlee never felt the way she believed Clay seemed to in that photo. She existed comfortably in her own skin, but confident? Not so much.

"Do you think he likes one of us?" Greenlee asked softly, hoping the interest he'd shown in her was a sign that they'd noticed too.

"Well . . . duh!" the girls said at the same time and giggled.

"That's a kinda stupid question, no offense."

"Err . . . okay," giggled Greenlee. "But do you think so, really? I don't even know him, you know what I mean?"

Marianne's turn: she grabbed the laptop and clicked on her page. Her eyes sparkled and she smirked, indicating she was up to something. Audrey shoved her playfully and peered over her shoulder. Greenlee dove on top of Audrey just as Mrs. Granger poked her head in the room. It was as if she were looking back in time. They'd all grown up together, still giggling, piled up on the bed acting silly. She smiled, shook her head, and snuck away. Marianne went back to the laptop, fingers typing ninety-to-nothing.

Marianne – **New taco place, not bad, hanging with new friends, always good!**

The buzz around the locker room was the TGP. Clay had noticed that all of his teammates were participating and they were still excited about the whole thing. Sweet! Clay finally had some kind of approval from A.J., the team leader, and now the others were following A.J.'s lead. Suggestions for Phase 2 had started to hit the site. Post after post, challenges, filled the page. Some were doable and some were idiotic. Starving after practice, the boys headed to their favorite fast-food restaurant and wolfed down burgers, but that didn't stop them from texting as they responded to each other's posts. One particular post appeared via Duckdog that caught everyone's attention; it was perfect, and as soon as Clay saw it, he knew it was a go! But who was Duckdog?

Duckdog – **Party Friday night at my house. Bring TGP. That's right, project invited!**
A.J. – **Second dat!**
Griff – **Third it . . . ha**
Tucker – **Ditto**

Quinton – **Post pics**
Clay – **Who's Duckdog?**
Clay – **Task accepted**
Clay – **Who's Duckdog?**
A.J. – **Don't know; cool user name**
Duckdog – **Haha . . . id . . . ?**
Duckdog – **Ya know me**
A.J. – **K if u say so**
Griff – **Spread the word**
Riley – **Done**
Clay – **Send details**
Duckdog – **K**
Duckdog – **Can Dozer join group?**
A.J. – **Who's Dozer?**
Duckdog – **He's cool, u'll like him**
A.J. – **Again, identity?**
Duckdog – **Ha u know him**
A.J. – **Yes, OK then**
Duckdog – **K, I'll tell him**
Quinton – **Second dat**
Whoozer – **Third dat**
Clay – **Who's Whoozer?**
A.J. – **Dunno**
Clay – **K**

Still pumped from the responses to his project, Clay headed home.

"Are you hungry, son?" Wes Monning called from the living room.

Clay dropped his bag on the kitchen floor and leaned over the countertop. He'd just eaten, so no, he wasn't. Instinctively his mom grabbed the bag that he'd just set down and started to pull out his wet workout clothes from earlier that day. She handed him a fresh set and headed for the laundry room. Clay repacked his bag and went into the living room. His dad was sitting on the couch, waiting for him to come home. Clay looked forward to their visits as they sat on the couch every night talking about every detail that Clay could remember from his practice. What he'd done right or wrong and everything that the coach had discussed with the team. His dad tried to interpret the coach's comments to help decipher what he had meant. Helping his son utilize his talent and position was their time together. Clay rubbed his face in his hands. He was tired; his dad noticed and insisted he go on to bed.

"You need your rest, son. Did you have time to finish your homework?"

He still had a tiny bit left to do, but he could manage, he said.

"Well go on, then," his dad said proudly, patting his son on the back. "Get on with your bad self, as they say," he winked. "Get it done and get to bed. Like I said, you need your rest!"

Clay grinned, leaned in, and hugged him. He kissed his mom on the cheek and said good night.

* * *

The three girls were sitting on the floor in Greenlee's room when a quiet ding caught their attention.

"OMG, look what I just got," Greenlee said excitedly.

Greenlee peered over Marianne's shoulder.

"Oh crap! Click it, hurry!" Audrey said excitedly.

Marianne grabbed Audrey's hand just in time.

"No, stop! Wait a minute. Eeeeeek, seriously, I'm freaking!"

Blank stares at the laptop. Friend request, Clay Monning, complete with message attached. *Hey Greenlee girl, ☺ let's talk.*

"*OMG!*" Greenlee giggled. "What do I do?"

"Seriously . . . Greenlee girl? Whatever!" Marianne said sarcastically.

"Ah . . . Marianne, admit it, come on, that's kinda cute," Audrey said, laughing. "I wish someone, you know who, would give me a cute nickname." She nudged Greenlee, "You think he's cute too, right?"

"What do you think he wants to talk about?" Greenlee asked. "And yes, kinda, I guess, yes, weird maybe, but cute!"

"He just likes you, that's all," Audrey said in between laughs. "Add him already; maybe his friend will add me."

Greenlee continued to hesitate, so nervous she couldn't move and once again she reread the message out loud. *Hey Greenlee girl, ☺ let's talk.* Clasping her hand over her mouth, she read it one more time to herself. *Hey Greenlee girl, ☺ let's talk.*

"OMG, Greenlee girl, that's so cute, right?"

Marianne was the only one that seemed to think the new name was annoying, rolling her eyes, and shaking her head. She managed a fake smile on behalf of her friend, who after all seemed overly excited about the ridiculous way he'd addressed her. Audrey grabbed Greenlee's hand and before Greenlee realized what was happening dropped it on the return key. Uncontrollable laughter took over as soon as they realized that she'd just accepted the friend request, and the girls waited to see if he'd respond. Within seconds the accepted notification flag popped up, and Clay immediately posted on her page.

"OMG, what do I do?" Greenlee asked. "Should I post something in response?"

Clay – **Thanks for the add Greenlee girl** ☺
Greenlee – **Yep**
Clay – **Watz up?**
Greenlee – **Nothing**
Greenlee – **U**
Clay – **Same**
Greenlee – **Ur welcome btw**
Clay – **what?**
Clay – **Oh the friend add, k**

Greenlee pointed to the screen and waited for the girls' guidance. Clay stared at his laptop and grinned. Her profile photo was some club pic. You had to really search to find her. She must not want to be found, he thought. He stared at it for a while, and then hit the private message button. He wanted to send a clear but subtle message with no red flags that would leave the door open.

Clay – **Well, like I said, cool name! Had fun hanging at lunch, new here & everything. Talk 2U later**

Laurel noticed that Clay and Greenlee were now friends on Teens2teens. Livid IMs flew back and forth, along with the appropriate friend requests and adds. If Greenlee was friends with Clay, then she was going to be friends with Clay and with all his friends. Clay hit accept right away and so did every other dude. It never crossed Clay's mind that Laurel had sent that request because she'd seen him add Greenlee. It didn't occur to him that adding both girls at the very same time would be an issue. Laurel was hot, he liked her; adding her was easy. Greenlee was a project; Laurel was the girl he was interested in. She made him smile, just thinking about her. Laurel, what a pain in the butt! He liked that she irritated him. Nothing worse than a boring girl! The message alert sound startled him.

Greenlee – **BTW thnx 4 driving today**
Clay – **Yarrr**
Greenlee – **CYA**
Clay – **K**

The party suddenly crossed Clay's mind. Could he get her to come? There's only one way to find out, so he asked her.

"OMG, look," Marianne pointed to the screen.

Clay – **Party Friday night, wanna go?**

Greenlee stared at the message. Clay flipped on his TV and waited for her to reply. It took a few minutes longer than he'd expected, but he finally got his answer. His next entry was a post on the TGP page, complete with another unflattering photo that Greenlee had no idea had been taken. Caption: *Gross & btw . . . yes Duckdog, TGP will be there on Friday.*

Clay – **Call me Golden, mission accomplished, Phase 2 in motion**
Tucker – **WTH dude, awesome**
Duckdog – **Guess she's coming?**

Clay – **Yep**
A.J. – **is the hot girl going?**
Griff – **Tell her to bring the other one 2**
Clay – **Will do**
Clay – **Which hot girl, L?**
A.J. – **Yeah**
Clay – **She can**
Duckdog – **Everyone's invited**
Quinton – **Send details**
Duckdog – **Will do**
Dakota – **Post pics**
Riley – **Who's Duckdog**
Ryan – **Cool name**
Duckdog – **Thnx**

The comments were flying and the kids who had been observing but hadn't been participating were now joining in. Greenlee's conversation in the truck had been played over and over again, and her voice had even been manipulated into its own talking Emoji, which had also been shared with the team and on the site. Greenlee had practically become a cartoon character overnight; she had no idea, and slowly but surely the TGP page on the Teens2Teens site was becoming a very popular page to visit.

How was she going to pull off getting out of the house? Her parents would never let her go to a party, especially with a guy they'd never met. She didn't even know him. What was she thinking? That was the problem: she wasn't!

"Do you know what you're wearing tomorrow?" her mom asked. "I don't want any drama in the morning."

What was she going to wear? Immediately texts went out and responses came back, almost as fast as she'd sent them. It was decided that Marianne would lend Greenlee her favorite shirt. Paired with Greenlee's capris and *voilà* she had an outfit. Sleep was the furthest thing from her mind. Clay Monning . . . um . . . now he was consuming her thoughts. Not good.

Chapter 18 – Two at a Time

Ideas for next phase of *The Greenlee Project* covered the page. Clay had his pick, and he couldn't be happier. The boys joked about it as they drove to school, talking about the popularity of the page. People were posting bets to see how quickly Clay could complete each task that he had been assigned or agreed to take on. New people were being added; most were being screened, but not all. Clay's phone vibrated in his pocket and he handed it to Tucker, who read the message out loud to the entire truck of guys. Clay blushed, but acted as if he wasn't embarrassed.

JUST SAYING HI ☺

"Well at least it's from the hot chick," Riley laughed. "Could have been from the other girl."

It gave A.J. an idea. He should get her number next, text her, and then Clay could text and post their messages.

"Brilliant, even if I do say so myself," A.J. said laughingly.

"Yeah, I should've thought of that already," Clay admitted. "But no worries! It will give me something to talk about with her later today."

Griff – **Golden getting digits. Stay posted.**

Griff tapped his watch. They all knew what that meant: time was ticking; the boys thought it was hysterical. He should've known this was getting out of hand, but he didn't listen to his gut. Grabbing Clay's phone, Griff answered Laurel's text. Clay laughed. A.J. answered the next one. A few texts went back and forth, but then one message came through that made them all laugh.

Laurel – **This so isn't Clay . . . What ev . . . see ya!**

A.J. read the text out loud. Clay died laughing. That Laurel was no dummy.

"Dude, if you *don't* go for her, I am. Hot and smart, I like it!" A.J. threw the phone back at Clay. "Seriously dude, I'll back off until you don't step up. Then you're toast!"

They parked, grabbed their stuff, and headed to their lockers. Clay's mind was on Laurel. He liked her. He'd make a move. How he was going to do that, he didn't know. Greenlee or Laurel? He would chase Laurel and keep up with the TGP, or whatever, and figure it out. How'd she get his number, anyway? Dang it, that made him smile again!

"How'd she get my number anyway, that's the second text I've gotten from her."

"Dude, really? Stop complaining?"

"Nahhh . . . I like that girl!"

"Gonna say . . . like I said, if you don't ask her to the party, I will!"

Both girls! Okay. Griff's fingers were tapping ninety to nothing on his phone, and Clay knew that he must be making another post. Everyone around him responded, including A.J. Clay, reading the posts over their shoulders, laughing, added his own responses. Looking down the hallway, trying to spot TGP, but he didn't see her. Getting her digits at this point was an essential move, mandatory in order to continue the game, but he wasn't worried. *Piece of cake*, he thought. Now he had to make sure Laurel was at the party. That's the girl he really wanted to hang with. Posts about the two girls being at the same party, one Laurel, the other being the project, filled the screen. Laurel was never named. Hot chick, that's what they called her. Golden brings two; two at a time . . . that's our boy.

"We don't know for a fact that they'll both be able to make it," Clay said, pointing to Griff's last post.

"But we don't know that they won't," Griff replied.

Clay had plenty of time to ask both of them and figure out a way to get them there. His mind was racing as he tried to work out different scenarios in his head. A.J. nudged Tucker, who shoved Clay, startling him.

"Earth to Golden . . . dude, waz up?" Tucker asked.

Clay grinned as he shoved Tucker back into A.J. "Nothing dude, just looking for TGP's numbers. Got to get this posting stuff done, you know what I mean?" he grinned.

"Hey, you have my respect, Golden, now anyway." Tucker looked around the hall, leaned in, and mumbled under his breath where no one could hear him but Clay. "Leave it to me, my friend and don't say I never did anything for you. Give me a minute."

Tucker disappeared and A.J. shrugged his shoulders. "I don't know what he's doing, dude."

Clay was contemplating telling Laurel about the project if she saw him talking to Greenlee. He was nervous about that and didn't know what to do.

"Dude, you're acting weird. What's wrong with you?"

Clay reconsidered it as soon as A.J. asked him what was wrong.

"Nothing. Like I said, I'm just ready to get on with it, that's all."

Tucker reappeared. "You're welcome."

"What?" Clay asked.

"Hot girl, she'll be there. TGP is your problem."

Well, that was easy, thought Clay. "What'd you do?"

Tucker was laughing. "Told her that you wanted her there. That's true, you do. So we're good." He grinned at Clay. "You just text her the details. I told her you'd do that!"

Duckdog – **Details: 4907 W. Taylor Ct. 7pm – when ev**
A.J. – **BThere**
Griff – **Ditto**
Tucker – **2nd Dat**
Quinton – **Beer?**
A.J. – **Really? Stupid!**
Quinton – **Just asking**
Duckdog – **I didn't see anything, ha**

Wheezer – **Fake i.d. got one**
A.J. – **Who's Wheezer?**
Duckdog – **He's cool**
A.J – **Again, who's Wheezer**
Griff – **Cool name**
Clay – **No beer! Coach–**
Quinton – **Just asking**
Duckdog – **Didn't see anything**
Wheezer – **hahahahaha**
Tucker – **Where's the hot girl?**
Riley – **Got TGP's Digits?**
Clay – **On it**
A.J. – **Get on it!**
Dakota – **hahaha . . . get on it**
Clay – **Not**
Clay – **Greenlee girl ☺ how about them digits?**

He had no idea how long it would take for her to check the site; they had no classes together that day, so unless he ran into her, he'd be out of luck. Wanting to get her number, he wondered if he should ask her friends if he saw them first. Anxiousness was setting in, starting to make his skin feel prickly. Football was on his mind and this initiation was starting to feel like a chore. He wanted to be a part of the team. He was ready to play football again.

Tucker was right: he did actually like A.J. He really wasn't a bad person and it was his senior year. He wanted to play football, to his keep his position. The scholarship offers were coming in and Clay understood that. He knew that he'd have plenty of playing time next season, and he was still playing some this season. Next year he'd start for sure! He caught a glimpse of Laurel. She was with her friends, as usual, laughing, digging in her purse. She looked good, she always did. He looked down just as she caught sight of him, but she wasn't going to let him off the hook that easily. His phone vibrated in his pocket, and he couldn't help but grin when he read her text. That girl wasn't shy!

Laurel – **You're a snob?** ☺
Clay – **Yep . . . U?**
Laurel burst out laughing as she typed her reply.
Laurel – **Well I didn't expect that**
Clay – **Looking forward to Friday, glad ur going**
Laurel – **I know**
Clay – **U know?**
Laurel – **Ur glad I'm going** ☺
Clay – **lol—later**
Laurel – **K**

"Who are you talking to?" Kelsey asked.

"Hottie Clay. He's actually kinda funny," responded Laurel.

Kelsey and Brittany huddled around Laurel, giggling, as they read his texts.

Clay's next text was completely unexpected. It was short and to the point, but Laurel squealed so loudly that both girls jumped up and grabbed the phone out of her hand.

"Look at my text. OMG read it."

Clay – **Can I call you?**
Laurel – **Yes**
Clay – **K— Later, again**
Laurel – ☺ **K**

"Party this Friday night ladies. Start planning!" Marianne instructed.

Plans had to be made in advance to ensure the optimum late night hours needed. The sleepover for this one would have to be at Audrey's. If they were lucky, her mom would work the third shift; if not, then second shift at the hospital wouldn't be too bad, but either way, Audrey's house on Friday night was a must.

IMs back and forth, and calls between parents verified that an actual sleepover, movie, and pizza night were really taking place. One tiny detail that the girls didn't share was that Audrey's mom was working the third shift and wouldn't be home. They would look up a great movie they'd eventually see, memorize details, skip movie, go to the party, have a great time, and of course last but not least, order pizza so the empty box would be there. They'd be hungry by then anyway. They had no idea, as excited as they were, that what was about to transpire was going to be disastrous. Their thoughts went no further than the clothes they'd wear and the guys they liked who would be there, and the fact that they were invited in the first place.

Laurel hit send, and then threw her phone on the bed. The constant receipt of messages kept it buzzing, but there was only one text she was waiting for. She had time to jump in the shower since Clay was still on the field anyway, and she already knew that he'd text her when he was done. Her text was but a tease.

Laurel – **Hurry up already**

Presumptuous? Sure it was, but that was part of Laurel's charm. She knew that he'd text her back, but that didn't stop her from checking her phone a time or two. They'd already talked twice that day. When she came out of the shower Brittany was sitting on her bed.

"Hey, your mom wanted to know if you needed anything." She hesitated, "Are you hungry or something?"

"Gag, and no!" Rolling her eyes, she threw the wet towel from her hair on the floor and screamed down the stairs, "Quit trying to feed me already! I told you I ate before you got here. I was starving." Laurel raised her hands in disgust. "Are you kidding me? Geez already, wt . . ." She stopped in mid-sentence, her mother standing before her and even Brittany wondered how in the heck she got there so fast!

"Watch your mouth young lady and I'm not having this conversation with you again. Something is amiss and I haven't figured it out yet, but I will. You're losing too much weight and I don't know why. Keep it up and we're going to see Dr. Novellea."

Immediately on the defensive, Laurel stared down Brittany, eyes flashing. She started to raise her voice but the sound of a text coming in, likely from Clay, reminded her to keep her mouth shut or at least her tone down, or she'd be grounded for sure. Friday night's party was on the horizon and she didn't want to blow that!

"OMG, Mom, seriously! I ate for real. I'm *not* lying to you." Laurel thought briefly about her words and said the next thing that popped into her head, regretting it as soon as she'd said it. "If you like, we'll have dinner tomorrow, okay, together I mean. I won't eat when I get home, I'll wait for you."

Her mom smiled; at least then she could monitor her and see what she was really eating. It seemed to pacify her, although the thought of having to sit down and consume an entire meal made Laurel nervous. What if she looked fat in the outfit that she'd planned to wear Friday? *OMG* she thought, the pressure was too much!

"That would be lovely. I'd enjoy that." Satisfied with her suggestion, her mom left the room.

"We're here to help, Laurel. We're really worried, too. Are you okay, really?" Brittany asked. "It's getting weird, Laurel, noticeable, you know what I mean?"

"Okay, I'm going need you to shut up now, 'cause that's just stupid and look," she said pointing to her phone, "Clay's just texted me back and look what he said."

Brittany read the text and smirked. "You are always the lucky girl!"

"I know, right?"

"Seriously, that's too obnoxious even for you, Laurel." Brittany, laughing, shook her head at Laurel's ridiculous look of disdain for the comment that she'd just made.

"I know," Laurel said, "I was just playing."

"Yeah right, whatever!"

Clay – **Pushy, like it** ☺
Laurel – ☺ **Ur slow, football I mean, practice**
Clay – **We're working. Can't wait till Friday**
Laurel – **Me 2**

For a split second Clay contemplated asking if she and her friends needed a ride, but then TGP came to mind and he caught himself just in time. Shaking his head, he let out a sigh. Suddenly hanging with Laurel seemed a lot more fun than pursing TGP on behalf of the team. Resentfully and with a great deal of hesitation, he sent the next text to Greenlee.

Clay – **Still going?**
Greenlee – **Yes**
Clay – **Cool, meet ya there**
Greenlee – **K**
Clay – **Later, Greenlee girl** ☺
Greenlee – **Ha!**

Greenlee stared at the text. She couldn't believe he had just confirmed that he would meet her at the party. She smiled as she typed. Of course she was going, come hell or high water, but she didn't have to let him know that. A simple response to his was enough. After the text was sent, she buried her face in her pillow. She could barely contain herself. Legs kicking, squealing though muffled, delirious and giddy didn't begin to describe how happy she felt. Friday couldn't get there soon enough for Greenlee! If only she'd known what Clay had in store for her and the others, she never would have given him the time of day. As she lay in bed, she wondered what she would say to him or how to talk to him without sounding like a total idiot. She had no idea what to talk about.

Clay lay in bed wondering how he could impress Laurel. That jet-black hair that she had, that smirk that knocked him off his feet, and that attitude he hadn't quite figured out, not to mention the fact that he knew she liked him, too, had him reeling. Greenlee crossed his mind. What an inconvenience. That *Greenlee girl, awww*, he thought, *what do I do about her?*

Chapter 19 - Party

Every guy on the team knew Duckdog. It was like he'd said—except the boys knew him as Duncan, one of the trainers that they saw in the locker rooms, sidelines, and generally everywhere during football season. A.J. cracked up as soon as he saw him. Griff grabbed him, picked him up, and squeezed him bear-hug style.

"Duckdog, ya had me! I had no idea that was you—now, tell me, how many of your other friends did you add to the T G P?"

He grinned and replied, "Just a few, but they won't say anything."

"Nice one dude!" Griff laughed, "I meant it by the way, cool name!"

"I told ya you knew me!"

Duckdog's house was tucked away on the outskirts of town. Although it was a gated community, that didn't matter because Duckdog had pasted the code on the box. It lasted until the neighbors found out and took it down, but it didn't stop the kids from getting in, because texts were sent with the code. Other than that, it was the perfect location for a party, especially an unsupervised teen party. Greenlee had never even been to a real teen party before, let alone an unsupervised one.

"Are you sure this is where you're supposed to be? It looks, well, fancy or something," asked Marianne's sister.

Marianne had bribed her sister for a ride and it had cost her twenty bucks for gas—and an extra twenty to keep her mouth shut—but it was worth it. Their first teen party and they had another cool teen to drop them off.

"Yeah, it's the right place. You saw the sign on the gate," Marianne said, laughing. "Party at Duckdog's."

"Hey," her sister hollered as the girls got out of the car, "if you can find a ride home, great, but if you can't, you better call me! Mom will freaking kill me if I lose you three!" She pulled away, but stopped halfway down the driveway. Something didn't seem right. Maybe it was because it was her kid sister or maybe it was because . . . she didn't know. Her phone began ringing and changed everything. It reminded her of her own party she was supposed to attend. She rolled down the window and yelled again.

"It will make my life so much easier if you can find a ride and get yourselves home, but if you can't, call me. Trust me: I mean that! But be home by twelve. I'm not getting busted for you!"

The three of them were standing outside the door to the party.

"Who's gonna ring the bell?" Greenlee asked.

Marianne shook her head. "Oh my God, seriously? It's a freaking party, people! Smile already, ugh."

"I think I'm gonna puke!"

"Greenlee, you're fine," Marianne said, dismissing her comment. "Just relax. My sister's been going to these things since she was our age. It'll be fine."

Reluctantly Greenlee knocked on the door. No answer. She rang the bell, still no answer. Laughter and voices penetrated through the walls, Marianne opened the door and started to walk into the house. Audrey and Greenlee's feet were planted firmly on the doormat.

"Trust me, they're expecting people just to walk in. Like I said, it's a party!"

A massive kid suddenly appeared, startling Greenlee and Audrey. Marianne continued to walk into the house as if she'd been there a million times. Greenlee and Audrey stood patiently at the door, waiting for an invite to enter the house. Not sure what to do, they stood like two deer caught in headlights.

"Did you need something?" he asked the two girls.

"Um . . . " a startled Greenlee managed to say.

"Whoa, okay then," the kid laughed. "I'm going to get something out of my car, so you guys go on in."

Greenlee looked the guy up and down, but her eyes went back to one thing—his neck. It was huge.

"Dude, you're massive!" said Greenlee.

He laughed at her, which surprised her. She couldn't take her eyes off him. His neck was thick. He was cute, tall, fit, and it dawned on her he must be one of Clay's teammates; surely he was a football player too.

"I get that a lot. Down the hall," he pointed. "Help yourself to whatever you can find in the kitchen. Gotta warn ya, pickings are slim. The guys are always hungry, if you know what I mean." He grinned and walked past them. "My casa is your casa as they say. By the way, I'm Daniel, Duncan's twin and Duckdog's bro."

"Oh my God, there's two of them, two!" Audrey squealed after Daniel walked away. "Two!" She pointed to Marianne and then to herself. "Two of them. So one for you and one for me!"

"Hey, what about me?"

"Forget it girl, you've got Clay. Those two are ours." Audrey squeezed Greenlee's arm. "Just kidding. You can have one if you want—I don't even know him. I probably wouldn't like him anyway," girl code for "he probably wouldn't give me the time of day."

Greenlee scoped out the room. She was looking for one person and one person only: Clay. She caught sight of him nestled in a corner, surrounded by a group of people, guys and girls, laughing and joking. His laughter rang out above the rest and Greenlee recognized it immediately—laughter from his gut. Whatever they were talking about was entertaining. His dark hair moved each time he bobbed his head. She caught glimpses of his eyes every now and then and even from there, they were sparkling. Observing him from a distance was kinda interesting—watching him having fun with his friends, knowing that he had no idea he was being watched. *Stalker. OMG . . . I'm a freaking stalker.* Greenlee thought. *Okay, but I do have to quit talking to myself, 'cause that's just crazy!* She came back to reality when Marianne poked her in the ribs.

"Let's get a drink," Marianne suggested.

Greenlee waved them on but stayed put, afraid to lose her cherished spot—she had a perfect view and she wasn't about to give it up. She causally glanced around the room. Most of the faces she did not recognize, but that didn't matter. These kids weren't the ones she'd hang out with on a regular basis anyway. She didn't know them and they didn't seem too interested in getting to know her or her friends. Her eyes ran over the tops of heads and back to the group of kids in the corner—Clay's group. He was leaning toward one person in particular, laughing, whispering, and having a great time. Greenlee stared, still wondering whom that person was who was blocked from view. It must be a close friend of his, she thought.

Clay wiped his mouth with the back of his hand and then wiped his hand on the leg of his jeans. Classic dude move, Greenlee thought, and couldn't help but smile. Her smile disappeared as soon as he took a step backward, leaving a gap just large enough for a sneak peek at the person who appeared to have captivated the boy who had captivated her—she turned away as fast as she could, suddenly having a sick feeling in the pit of her stomach.

"Look, there's Clay," whispered Audrey, who was now standing at Greenlee's side. "OMG," she clamped her mouth shut and put her hands over it. She handed Greenlee a cup and asked, "Did you know that she was coming?"

Greenlee avoided eye contact with Audrey for fear that she might tear up. Feeling awkward and stupid, she shook her head and took a sip of the unknown liquid in her hand.

"Ew . . . what is that?" she asked and scrunched up her face. She took another sip of the nasty contents of the red plastic cup. It was bitter and burned going down.

"This tastes terrible. What did you say it was, seriously?"

"I didn't, but it's punch or something—dunno." Audrey shrugged, "Do you see how close he is to Laurel?"

"What?" Greenlee asked, knowing exactly how close he was sitting next to her. She was the girl he was captivated with. Greenlee, feeling slighted, turned toward her friends.

"You wanna get outta here?" Marianne asked, noticing Greenlee had turned white as a sheet. "I can call my sis. She can pick us up now instead of later."

"I thought he was kinda inviting Greenlee to this thing, didn't you?" Audrey asked, but the *wth are you thinking* look that Marianne shot her told her it was time to shut up. Audrey and tact didn't always go hand in hand.

"Well, at least he looks like crap," Marianne muttered under her breath and Greenlee managed a smile.

All three of them had a perfect view of Clay flirting with Laurel. Greenlee's heart sank as she watched him take the cup that Laurel was holding in her hand. She laughed, he laughed. She playfully shoved him, and he smiled and whispered something to her. She reached up and touched his face. Still holding the cup, he turned, and that's when he saw Greenlee. She was certain that she'd seen a hint of disappointment in his eyes the second he caught sight of her, but suddenly, as if on cue, he smiled that massive smile of his and walked toward her.

"Hey there, Greenlee girl, glad you could make it. Been here long?"

He didn't answer Laurel when she called after him. Maybe he hadn't heard her, or maybe he was too busy making a move on Greenlee. Laurel was ticked and Greenlee felt a panic attack coming on. Suddenly she had a desire to flee but had nowhere to go. A bright light took her by surprise. Marianne shoved Clay.

"WTH, seriously?" Marianne said protectively.

He laughed. "Chill, it's for the album, no one will ever see it." He held his phone up and showed the girls the pic. "See, it's Greenlee girl."

"Delete it," Greenlee snapped and grabbed at the phone. "That pic sucks!"

"And posted," Griff said, pointing to his phone since he'd snapped one at the same time of Clay snapping his picture.

A.J. posted a comment immediately:

A.J – **Game on!**
Duckdog – **Spiked the punch, if you know what I mean**
Quinton – **hahahaha**
Riley – **Pics**
Dustin – **how many can she drink**
Ernie – **Dude, that's wrong**
A.J. – **Who's Ernie?**
Ernie – **Duckdog added me**
Riley – **But how many do you think she can drink?**
Duckdog – **I know how many I can drink lol**

"Oh yeah, you guys remember Griff, right?" Clay pointed toward Griff as he walked toward them, wearing a grin from ear to ear. Just as Greenlee took a sip, snap. Another flash went off in her face.

"Seriously, enough with the pics!"

"It's all in fun. Here, you take some," Clay said and grabbed Griff's phone, handed it to Marianne, and of all things grabbed Greenlee and pulled her toward him. Greenlee spilled her drink, splashing some on her top, but that was nothing compared to the weirdness of being so close to Clay. Snap, pic, post.

"Good picture, I assume?"

It wasn't a real question. The sarcasm in Laurel's voice embarrassed Greenlee, forcing heat to rush to her cheeks, but the dim lights in the game room were her salvation. No one could see how embarrassed she was.

"Seriously . . . let me to take another pic of you two. Here, get closer."

She pointed to Greenlee in a belittling way. "What's your name again?" but she didn't wait for an answer. "Closer."

Clay scratched his face and mumbled under his breath before making a snide comment and faking unnecessary introductions. He liked Laurel, but she was about to mess it up.

"Not like you don't know each other, but whatever." He caught sight of Griff, who winked, and he knew that Griff was recording.

"Laurel, Greenlee. Greenlee, Laurel. Next."

"We've met," said Laurel.

Greenlee kept sipping her drink, which oddly appeared full again. Clay slung his arm around Greenlee and playfully pulled her cheek next to his. Greenlee felt a little more relaxed. Sipping the punch, which tasted better than it had before, Greenlee noticed that whatever was in the cup was going down nice and easy now, no bitter taste, and she definitely was starting to have fun. She even managed to laugh while Clay goofed around.

"Oh, I topped that off for you. You were drinking the punch, right?" Tucker said, while holding two more cups in his hands. He had topped off Audrey's and Marianne's drinks as well. "I know you're not driving, so you can drink this stuff. It's good for you," Tucker said with a laugh and everyone laughed with him except for Laurel, who was still miffed.

"Oh, here's your phone," Laurel hissed sarcastically, throwing it at Clay's head.

"Unnecessary," he hollered, but she'd already turned on her heels and stormed off.

"Dude, that's my phone," Griff said with a grin. "We've jacked up our phones. I must have yours."

Tucker's sudden interest in Greenlee made her feel uncomfortable. Marianne and Audrey were deep in their own conversation, and she desperately wanted to ask them if they could tell if Clay was worried that he'd ticked off Laurel. She couldn't remember if his eyes had followed Laurel down the hallway when she got mad. As she suspected, within minutes, he excused himself.

"Do you want some more?" Clay asked Greenlee.

"What?" She pointed upward but didn't know why. "The music, it's loud."

"Punch? Do you want some more punch?" Clay asked.

Audrey overheard the question, looked into Greenlee's cup, scrunched up her face, and responded on behalf of her friend.

"Stupid, look! Her cup is full."

Greenlee was horrified. "Audrey! You don't have to be rude."

She nodded and handed Clay her cup. If he wanted to chase after Laurel, that was fine. "Sure, freshen it up," she said, but as soon as he left she turned to Marianne and whispered, "I'm ready to go. Can you call your sister?"

"I'll try, but it's early and she's at another party. I know she won't come just yet. Relax. I'll get her." Marianne spoke softly. "It's just Laurel being Laurel. You know she has to be the center of attention." Pausing she added, "Look, if he wants to worry about Laurel, so be it. He has no idea what he's in for—she'll eat *him* for breakfast."

The girls giggled. That was true. Laurel would do just that. Audrey put her arm around Greenlee's shoulder and squeezed her, a show of support, but that didn't help. Tucker was back at their side. Why? The other guy, Griff, had never left. Why was he still there? The guy she liked was chasing after some other girl. Greenlee's stomach suddenly felt sick and everything inside of her told her to leave; yet against her better judgment, she stayed and forced herself to mingle with Clay's friends. She had no idea they were making posts about her as fast as their fingers could type. If she had, she wouldn't have been standing there.

Clay – **Great shot of TGP mouth open**
Duckdog – **Kill it**
Duckdog – **Not really dude, kill it, I mean**
Clay – **Gottcha, making video**

Griff – **Me 2**

Riley – **Post it**

A.J. – **Get her drunk, she's not driving**

Clay – **Pleaze 2 eazy**

Quinton – **hahahah**

Dirk – **LQTM (laughing quietly to myself) . . . money on Golden**

Clay – **Right . . . ha!**

A.J – **Epic fail ya mean**

Chapter 20 – Added the Girl

Clay waited for Laurel outside of the bathroom, and as soon as the door opened he grabbed her arm and pulled her toward a bedroom located on the opposite side of the hallway.

"What the hell," she said, but he noticed she didn't struggle. Her mouth was still going. "You must have mistaken me for that other girl, Greenlee. Clay, what in the hell do you think you're doing?"

"It's not what you think—I know it looks bad, but it's not what you think."

"Oh really! Well, you could've fooled me. I hate to sound cynical and all—but do I look stupid to you?"

She actually stopped to breathe, for which Clay was grateful, but when she took a deep breath, followed by an exhale, he knew she wasn't done with him yet. To his surprise, her voice had actually softened.

"I like you Clay, I do. But what's going on here? Do you really like that girl? I'm not going waste my time on you if you're interested in her." She shook her long dark hair over her shoulders, looking really cute doing it, scratched the tip of her nose and continued, "But seriously, her? Why her?"

Bold. She came right out and said it. She's not going to waste her time. A smile crossed Clay's face. She was jealous, and he liked it. He grabbed her hand and held it in his, his dark eyes locked on hers, and he noticed how beautiful her blue-green eyes were, even for a spoiled brat. The thought of her being a brat made him smile even more, and she gave him the oddest look.

Instinctively he grabbed her hand, pulled her toward him, and kissed her. She didn't stop him. He continued to hold her hand tightly in his.

"All I can say is this: it's really, really not what you think, and I really, really do like you."

Laurel took another deep breath and pulled her hand away. Obviously those were not the words she needed to hear. She took a step backward and rolled her eyes, folded her arms, and shook her head.

"What kind of explanation is that, Clay?"

It was Clay who felt nervous now and suddenly insecure. Maybe she didn't like him as much as he first thought. He was about to blow it with a girl he really liked, for the sake of a girl he didn't like. If he said too much, he'd blow it with the guys and fail his initiation. The whole TGP was not enough. He didn't want to blow it with Laurel. He grabbed her hand again and held onto it tighter than before, and this time when she tried to pull it away he wouldn't let her.

"Wait a minute, just wait a minute. Please, Laurel, a minute."

"You go out of your way to hang with her, invite her here knowing that I'm going to be here. I thought we were going to hang out. We're having a great time, but then you ditch me when she gets here, only to track me down and tell me that it's not what I think. Clay, exactly what is it? What am I supposed to think?"

"You're right! When you put it like that it sounds ridiculous; I know, but it really isn't what you think. I'm not interested in her at all. Laurel, I like you, not her."

He pulled her toward him and kissed her on the forehead. She still didn't believe the words that he had said, but she was confused. What was he trying to say?

"Try and trust me," he whispered. "Please. I do like you and I know this doesn't make sense right now, but whatever you hear or see tonight, it's truly, truly not what you think."

"Clay you're going to have to give me a little something more. I want to trust you, but you're going to have to trust me, too. That's fair isn't it? You trust me, I trust you?"

He hesitated but she moved forward and leaned her head on his shoulder. He wrapped his arms around her and against his better judgment he whispered, "I will say this, and I swear you can't tell a soul." She looked up at him, her eyes gleaming and he asked her again, "Laurel, you have to swear it, so much is riding on this."

"I swear Clay, I do. I really do. I swear it," she said quietly.

"It's a game, Laurel. This whole thing with that girl, Greenlee, is all part of a secret game, a very special game that you *can't* know anything about. And of course she doesn't know."

Laurel's face lit up as the pieces of the puzzle suddenly fell into place. It's a game. Greenlee is a game. Clay, the team, and all the attention poured on her. Of course there had to be more to it than Clay had said, but suddenly falling for a girl like that . . . this was starting to make sense. A wicked little grin formed on her beautiful pink lips and a throaty laugh that she could barely contain slipped from her mouth.

"Tell me more! Tell me all about it, please Clay, please."

He grinned and shook his head. Pleasing her pleased him, and he'd made her very happy.

"I promise I will fill you in later, but I can't yet. When the time is right, I'll give you all the details. I'll tell you everything."

He pecked her on the cheek and noticed how quickly her entire demeanor had changed. She was happy, smiling, content in the fact that his feelings for Greenlee were not genuine and that Greenlee was a joke in the eyes of the entire team.

"So, do you trust me?"

Laurel smiled and kissed him on his cheek. She nodded.

"I do trust you, but I think I could help you, if you can trust me. If I knew the extent of what you were up to, I could . . . "

The wheels in Clay's mind were turning. Should he tell her more? The sooner the task was done, the sooner he could spend time with Laurel. But not yet, it was still too soon and he knew that.

"I promise I'll fill you in as soon as I can, but don't worry, now you know why I'm acting so weird toward that Greenlee girl. You'll see in the long run why I had to do this."

"Can you tell me anything about the game, anything at all? Like is it a bet or something?"

He liked this girl; she didn't give up. She was persistent, like him. Clay chuckled, and shook his head.

"No," he laughed, "and you can't keep asking me that either. Deal?"

"No deal, but I'll try."

He hugged her tightly and she realized how strong he was; all the time he had spent in the weight room was definitely paying off. She watched him as he left the room; he turned around and winked at her. *So cheesy,* she thought, *but so hot!*

"Did you get lost?" Greenlee asked the second that Clay approached her and her friends. He handed her a drink.

"I have one, thanks," Greenlee said, glancing as inconspicuously as she could over his shoulder. Embarrassed that she'd sounded as bitchy as she had, she noted that Laurel was nowhere in sight and felt better, relieved. It would appear that he hadn't chased after her at all.

"Whoa, is something wrong?" He didn't wait for her to answer. Taking the cup she held in her hand, he replaced it with the one he held in his. "This one tastes better. Try it."

Greenlee felt hot, dizzy, and sick. She wasn't sure what this new feeling was. She hadn't felt like this before. She pushed it out of her head, intoxicated with Clay and unbeknownst to her, the punch. She glanced into the cup.

"What is this?" Greenlee asked.

"Duckdog's special' they're calling it. I haven't tried it yet, but they say it's good."

He took a sip and commented, "Yep, it's good, try it. By the way, I went to the kitchen to get drinks. Is there a problem? You seem snippy or something." He grinned. "Hey, do you want to get some air?"

Grabbing her hand, he led her toward the door and without hesitation she followed him. Greenlee recognized that it was unusual behavior for her. Justifying the exit by telling herself she truly needed air, she continued to follow him. The punch he had given her didn't taste too bad after all, and was better than the other stuff she'd been drinking. Some guy opened the door; she remembered hearing Clay's voice.

"Thanks, man," he said as she stumbled through it.

Griff, Tucker. A.J., Duckdog, and the others had followed Clay out the door, but several other guys and girls were already outside. Laurel, lo and behold, suddenly appeared with the BP.

Marianne shoved Audrey toward the back door. "Party just moved outside and we're tagging along," she instructed.

"Right. Sorry, wasn't thinking," Audrey giggled. "Duckdog's stuff is really good."

"Yeah about that . . . slow down. This is clearly spiked."

"What? What do you mean?"

"Seriously, Audrey? Get a clue!"

"OMG Marianne you must be right, cause I feel gooooooooood! Oh crap . . . that can't be good!"

"Ya think! Look at me, being the responsible one. Come on! Greenlee's out of her comfort zone and she just doesn't know it yet."

Every two seconds Clay was introducing her to someone he knew and photos were being taken: group shots, couple shots. Greenlee was on flash overload and quite frankly it was making her nauseous. It was so weird. Snap and post. Snap, flash. Snap, flash, post.

"Geez, I had no idea guys were this picture-crazy," said Greenlee.

Clay laughed. "Dude, we love pics."

He grabbed her face and pulled it toward him, and even though she suddenly felt dizzy, she enjoyed his attention. She felt his warm lips linger on her cheek a tad too long, followed by another flash, but the sound of a familiar voice brought her back to reality.

"Enough with the stupid pics, already," said Marianne, who placed herself smack in the middle of the shot.

"Oh my God, what are you doing, you freak!" Greenlee laughed, hugging Marianne's neck as she grabbed at Clay's phone.

"Let me see the pic, Clay."

He didn't show it to her until after he'd posted it on the TGP site. The caption read: *this girl wants me bad!*

"You have to delete that, seriously. We'll be busted for sure," she pleaded, though her laughter didn't match the severity of what she was trying to say. "I mean, not you and me, I mean, me and my friends . . . we're not supposed to be here. Where did you post that anyway? Did you post that? Wait a minute, where did you post that?"

She was distracted by Laurel of all people. "Looks like your glass is empty, dear. Clay, her cup is empty."

"It is? Well, I guess I better fill it up."

Laurel grabbed the cup out of Greenlee's hand. "Nah, I'm going that way anyway," she said. "I'll get it." She smiled. "Great punch isn't it?"

"What's with Laurel?" Marianne asked. "She's going to spit in it, bet me."

"She's trying to be friends. Is that so bad?" Clay responded. Hollering after Laurel, "Just bring back a pitcher."

Laurel waved, indicating that she'd heard his request, and would bring the pitcher, but first she tracked down the one person who could fill her in on what the plan was: A.J. Knowing him, it wouldn't take too long to get him to talk. She played him like Clay played Greenlee. He was walking toward her, trying to find Clay. It was perfect timing.

"Hey, you," he grinned. "Have you seen Clay?"

Laurel seized the opportunity, moved in for a hug, and started talking. A.J. hugged her back.

"As a matter of fact, I have. He's looking for you," she said, peering into his cup. Laurel took it out of his hand and took a sip. A.J. smiled. "Want me to fill that up for you?" she asked him.

"Nah," he said. "I got it. Want one?" He didn't wait for her to answer. "I do need to find Golden though, been looking for him. Where did you say he was, out back?"

She laughed, green eyes sparkling, and tossed her dark hair over her shoulders. "I didn't, but he is out back. Hang on a minute, though, I need to ask ya something."

A.J. took a drink from the red cup. "Oh yeah? What's that?"

"That girl, the Greenlee girl, he told me."

"I don't know what you're talking about," A.J. said unconvincingly.

Laurel smiled and leaned into his shoulder. "Sure you do; let's talk."

Grabbing his arm, she took a step forward. "In fact, let's get a couple of those cups while we're at it," she said and quit pulling his arm. He walked with her on his own. His mind was racing, trying to figure out what, if anything, she thought she knew.

"Relax, I'm here to help." She smiled and suddenly A.J. wasn't worried anymore.

The kitchen was packed with kids, but they managed to fill their cups. It was A.J.'s turn to grab Laurel's sleeve. Pulling her down the hall, he opened a bedroom door only to shut it again. With kids making out this was not exactly the place to talk, especially to discuss TGP.

"Dude!"

A.J. quickly opened the door again but quickly closed it again. "My mistake, keep it clean in there!"

He laughed, "We don't want to go in there, if you know what I mean."

Laurel giggled and reached for the door. A.J. stopped her and gently shoved her down the hall.

"No, no, wait a minute. Not like that, I didn't mean that they're doing anything, just making out, but still. Come on. Don't go in there. What if that was you?"

"My dad would kill me," she laughed. "Just kidding. I wasn't going in, I just want to talk to you."

A.J. smiled and pulled her into another room. Some kid was on the phone. As soon as he saw A.J., he pointed to the phone and mouthed the word *parents*. A.J. nodded. The kid said goodbye, hung up the phone, and left the room.

"So, tell me what it is you think you know," A.J. said with a grin.

Laurel sat on the edge of the bed. "I know all about the game, the one with Greenlee in it. But before you jump Clay, I figured it out on my own and made him tell me the rest. For the record, I think he's holding out on me." She was pretty insistent on that, and A.J. believed her.

A.J. walked toward the door but Laurel jumped in front of it, put her hands on his chest, which he found amusing, and told him to hang on. She had a plan too; one that could help them.

"Wait a minute; please, just wait a minute."

"Dude, Clay broke code. I'm pissed!" He didn't seem as mad as he pretended to be, but Laurel continued.

"It wasn't like that, A.J., I promise it wasn't. Seriously, I'm smarter than you give me credit for. I figured most of it out, nailed him on it, and like I said, he's holding out." Laurel started talking fast. "But I think I can help."

She looked A.J. in the eye. "A.J., think about this a minute. Clay hasn't even heard about this proposition yet. I'm talking to you as the team leader first."

"What proposition?" A.J. asked.

"I'm a girl, she's a girl. We share classes, locker space, showers after gym . . . "

A.J. was starting to get the picture but wasn't certain what Laurel had in mind. "Laurel, what exactly are you saying?"

A smirk crossed her lips, which turned into another throaty laugh. A.J. found himself laughing with her, too.

"What are you laughing at? Stop laughing and tell me what you're thinking," he said. "What is this so-called proposition that you're offering? You have my attention."

"It's perfect; think about it. Surely the punch," she pointed to his cup, "must have slowed you down."

A.J. grabbed her and pulled her toward him; thinking he was going to kiss her, she pulled away.

"You know I like Clay, right? Anyway, I want to help him. This Greenlee thing is a perfect way to do it."

A.J. stepped back, "Well, get on with it already. What is it?" He let go of her and waited for her to tell him.

"Add me to the group thing you guys have," she said, "*The Greenlee Project* page. Don't look so surprised: people are talking about it. I can help you with posts you couldn't dream of getting!"

Immediately he shook his head *no*. Swinging it like crazy back and forth, then to confirm he kept saying, "No, no, no, no way!"

"Wait a minute, seriously. Listen to me a second." She was persistent. "You don't have to use my name; I can use a fake one. But think about it A.J.: if you add me, I can ask her things and get her to say things that she'd never say to you or Clay or anyone else, except maybe her real friends." She kept talking, realizing that she had his attention.

"I can take pics and make posts as if I was a guy, one of your guys. Then you boys can leave your own comments. Seriously, think about it. Brilliant, isn't it?"

A.J.'s eyes started to get a little spark in them. Laurel was sure it could work. The more he thought about it, the more it made sense. She knew she had him when his face lit up. He finally got it; but it was going be risky, bringing in a girl. They wouldn't be able to tell anyone until it was over, except for Clay, because he was certain that she couldn't keep her mouth shut. A.J. knew that she'd tell him. But true, they could use a dude's name, and Laurel could post pics and comments that they couldn't dream of obtaining on their own. The possibilities were endless.

"You know, this is going go down in history. As the team captain, how cool would that be?"

"Pretty freaking cool!"

He downed the last of his drink and crushed the cup in his hand. Laurel laughed and downed hers.

"So what do you say?"

"With the exception of Clay, you have to swear not to tell anyone, not even your friends. You cannot say a word! You have no idea about this initiation stuff; we could all be kicked out of school or worse. This is serious stuff for our team, our families and friends, this brotherhood. Trust me, you don't get it, no offense."

"I get it."

A.J. took a deep breath, exhaled, rubbed his hand through his hair and said, "Well Larry43, welcome. I do agree that it would be wicked good. But I swear on your life, I will kill you if you ever breathe a word!"

"I swear I won't!" she laughed. "Larry43, I like it."

"Put it there," A.J. said extending his hand and Laurel took it. "I'm not saying that I'm threatening you or anything, but I am." He was grinning, "I swear if you spill, you will pay. I'll spill you."

"Let's get this party really started!" she said.

"Let's do it!"

The deal was made; her fake name added, a group message went out.

A.J. – **New member—TGP & Insta-post—Larry43**
Riley – **Who dat**
A.J. – **Friend of mine**
Riley – **K**

Laurel was giddy and pleased with herself, but had one more favor to ask of A.J. She stood right in front of him, staring up at him, her head all the way back just to see his face. She stepped back in order to make eye contact.

"Yessssss," he said, stringing out the *s*.

"Will you tell Clay for me?" A.J. shrugged at her and she could tell that he was confused by her request. Such a guy thing to do, not understanding that Clay might think that she may have stepped on his toes. "I just think it will come across better from you. It's such a great plan and like I said, I came to you. If it's your plan, he won't say anything. If it's my plan, he might think I'm intruding on your guy stuff—you know, like what you were talking about."

A.J. agreed. "I'll tell him. No problem. Now go make nice with your new best friend!"

Chapter 21 – Tonight's Entertainment: Greenlee

Clay was acting weird and his friends, people that Greenlee didn't know, were acting weirder than that. Lightheaded but still giggling, Greenlee had no idea that she was the reason they were acting so weird. Nearly everyone around her had their phones recording or taking pictures. Greenlee didn't have a clue. Laurel rejoined the group outside with a pitcher in hand. That was odd, considering her friends were not huddled around her, not to mention the fact that she was standing elbow-to-elbow with Greenlee. Clay got right in front of Greenlee's face and in an overly loud voice announced that he thought she was hot.

"I think you're kinda hot," he slurred.

"What?"

"Are you deaf? he said with a laugh. "I said I think you're kinda hot."

Laurel grinned. It was time to add her two cents. It was bitter and mean, but she loved it. She continued egging the conversation on. Clay had no idea that A.J. had added Laurel to the group. Laurel was now part of the project.

"He likes you, don't ya, Clay?"

Greenlee's head spun toward Laurel, her eyes fixated on hers, but Clay spoke again, and she turned back toward him.

"What did you say, Laurel?"

Greenlee couldn't decipher why Clay looked so weird. Clay didn't know if he was in trouble for saying that, or if Laurel really understood that he wasn't interested in Greenlee. Greenlee stood and observed both of them.

"Like her," Laurel repeated. "You said she was hot 'cause you like her, right?"

Greenlee was uncomfortable and Laurel loved it. Griff snapped another picture that depicted how uncomfortable she was. He posted it immediately. The caption was awful:

Golden, two chicks, one hot, one not!

Greenlee grabbed Marianne's arm. "I'm ready to go," she said. "I don't think I feel right. I'm going be sick."

"Are you okay?"

"No, I'm not," Greenlee whispered. "I feel sick."

Griff nudged Clay.

"Hey, look at her. She doesn't look good."

"Are you okay, Greenlee?" Clay asked.

Greenlee nodded. "Yeah, it's hot even out here, isn't it?"

"I didn't mean to embarrass you, I just think you're kinda of cute, that's all."

Greenlee blew her bangs out of her face, hoping her face had returned to normal. Squeezing Marianne's arm was the signal that she could hang a while longer. But Marianne had already started to dial her sister. Voice mail. She stepped away and left a detailed message.

"Kind of?" she said. "I'm kind of cute . . . that's rude." She managed a giggle. "Dip wad, you're supposed to say that I'm really cute." She was stunned that she'd insulted him, but didn't feel bad about it.

"Give me a break. I'm a guy."

Gag! Laurel rolled her eyes. Reaching over, she grabbed Clay and Greenlee's cups, excused herself, and left to refill them once again. If they didn't need a drink, she did. This was nauseating.

"I don't want another, Laurel. I'm good."

"Whatever, that's fine, but I do," and off she went.

"So how's football going?" Greenlee asked, not really caring but managing small talk.

"Way random. Where did that come from?" asked Clay.

Clay grabbed her hand; instinctively she pulled it away, which was funny to him. She was clearly uncomfortable, which was perfect since he was recording the whole thing. Clay's newfound power, so effortlessly obtained, heightened the intensity of the game. Reaching for Greenlee's hand, he placed hers in his as she squirmed, but he held her even tighter. Laurel stepped back out onto the patio and handed them each a cup. Greenlee declined. Laurel downed Greenlee's drink.

"New batch," she stated, turned on her heels, and went back into the house. She knew the game but she didn't have to watch it unfold.

"What's her problem?" asked Greenlee.

"Dunno. I'll go find out."

"I don't think so!" Greenlee objected. "Stay right here."

"Relax, I'll be right back. Besides, she likes you, too. You guys could be friends."

Clay followed Laurel into the house, sneaked up behind her, and wrapped his arms around her waist. She jumped. Realizing it was Clay, she relaxed and leaned backward into his chest.

"You jerk! I don't want to watch that crap."

"Wait a minute, it's not what you think, remember?"

"Well, you're being pretty convincing. I'm still not watching it. It's making me want to vomit." She turned around and motioned for him to join her in the bedroom. She shut the door, leaned toward him, and kissed him: a deep, passionate kiss.

"I have a surprise for you," she said slyly. "You're either going to love it or hate it, but remember it's all in the name of the game."

"Oh really, and what is it?"

"I know."

"You know what?"

Laurel started laughing, which made Clay laugh as well. Between the punch, the information that she had to offer, and the knowledge that she could help destroy Greenlee and help elevate Clay's respect with the team, she was beside herself with glee.

"Come on already," he said and grabbed her waist. He sat down on the edge of the bed and pulled her down onto his lap. "Tell me, what is it?" Then he looked at her and grinned. "Uh oh, tell me what you did."

She started laughing. "I know."

"You know what?"

"I know about *the project*." She hesitated only for a second, then the words tumbled out of her mouth in such a way that Clay was temporarily stunned. Speechless, he sat there with his mouth wide open.

"I know about Greenlee, the initiation, the page, *The Greenlee Project* page, everything." Pecking his cheek and holding his face, she kissed his lips softly and whispered, "A.J. told me everything; well kinda. You can thank him later, but isn't this great?"

"He did what?" Clay screeched, jumped up, and steadied Laurel on her feet. "He told you about the initiation and TGP? Everything, for real?"

His brown eyes suddenly stared intensely at Laurel. His hand wiped beads of sweat from his brow, unsure of what to do or say next.

"Let get me this straight: A.J., team captain, told you, a girl, about our top-secret initiation?"

"Well, kinda." Laurel's eyes shot downward. "I sort of helped him along, tricked him just a bit."

"What the hell are you talking about Laurel?" Clay snapped. "Spill!"

Laurel chose her words carefully. "Well, I knew something was going on. You had told me most of it, without telling me the details. I kinda led A.J. to believe I knew more than I really did," her voice trailed, as she kissed Clay's cheek. "Then he really told me himself, well, after he thought you had shared some, not all, just some of it."

Clay wasn't sure how to react. Relieved. Angry. Confused. What next?

Diverting Clay's attention from blame back to the game, Laurel whispered, "A.J. did have a brilliant idea." He stared at her as if she'd lost her mind, as if A.J. had lost his mind. "Clay, it's perfect," she said softly. "A.J. thinks I can help you."

"Come again?"

Laurel kissed him on the cheek and threw herself back into his arms. "I know, it's crazy but it's priceless!"

"Explanation please; dead confused right now!" Clay grabbed her shoulders, sat back down, and placed her once again in his lap. "From the beginning, tell me everything."

Laurel explained her version of what she wanted Clay to think. Once she was done, she waited for his response. It was as she hoped: perfect.

"This is awesome!"

"I know!"

"Have you captured anything yet?" he asked. "I mean anything girlie good?"

She nodded. "Well, kinda; I've been loading up that punch, the trashcan stuff she's been drinking. I would feel bad for her but everyone's been drinking it and she likes it. I didn't force her to drink it. She was talking about your eyes. Barf. She also said that she thought you were really hot and she wanted to kiss you."

He laughed. "That's cool. She also said that she liked the punch when I gave some to her, too." Clay lifted his cup. "It is good."

"We better get out there, though, you know what I mean? She'll come looking. She already got snippety when she thought I was with you earlier."

Clay gently shoved her off of his lap. "You know I'd rather stay here with you, right? You do know that? Once this is over, you and me."

Laurel smiled, gloating over the fact that she had Clay. She leaned over and kissed him again.

"I do know that, and you should be with me!"

"See. That's what I like about you: you're confident and beautiful. I'll stop making an ass out of myself now. But you know what I mean."

"I do," she said and her green eyes sparkled. "Okay, save some compliments for later. I like them. Let's get of here and find *your girl*."

Clay rolled his eyes and kissed her one last time, then headed toward the door.

Marianne, Audrey, and Greenlee were pretending not to notice that Clay had taken so long. They had no idea what Griff was talking about, but at least they pretended to care. Griff, Tucker, and A.J. were trying to engage them in conversation so that they wouldn't leave the party just yet. They'd heard Marianne leaving messages for her sister and evidently her sister still hadn't responded. They liked the attention, even though they couldn't care less about cars. They were having fun just hanging with each other and the guys. So who cared if the topic of conversation happened to be something that didn't interest them? Greenlee's eyes searched the other kids as they walked back and forth through the yard. She was looking for Clay as she continued to slam down drinks. Marianne filled up their cups, skipping Greenlee's. Greenlee didn't object. Everyone, including Greenlee, was feeling the effects of the mysterious punch. She'd had enough. Snacks had run out, but pizza had been delivered. Every kid had coughed up some money to contribute to the cost of the pies. Greenlee nibbled on a slice of cheese pizza. It seemed to help settle her stomach a little bit.

"Where's the bathroom?" Audrey asked.

"What?"

"The bathroom?"

Griff laughed. "Oh yeah, dude, that way." He pointed toward the house and explained, "Through the kitchen, down the hall, and on the left."

A.J. walked toward her. "You need a hand, or two." He laughed at his own joke, and as if on cue, the boys laughed with him.

"She's fine, thank you, but hell no!"

Marianne grabbed Audrey. "I'll go with you." They started to walk toward the French doors. "Hey, Greenlee, you coming?"

She wasn't going anywhere. Clay was at her side, fawning all over her. Laurel had joined them again. Why was she always there and next to her? Simple, it was Clay! Greenlee wished that she'd leave, but it didn't seem to matter. Clay was standing right next to her, shoulder to shoulder. His arm had even slid around her waist, which made her smile. Laurel didn't look too happy and that made Greenlee ecstatic.

"Ah, I think I'm going puke. That's gonna be a Kodak crap moment, don't you think Griff?" said Laurel.

Griff heard his name and whipped out his phone.

"Ew. Why yes, Laurel, I think I agree." Snap. "Smile for the camera, Golden and Greenlee!"

A.J. winked at Laurel. Nice move. She was good. Laurel was very pleased with herself and knew that Clay would be too. Seizing the moment, she blurted out a comment that drove the crowd that had gathered around them crazy.

"One more for the album," she said. "Make it a good one, Clay. As they say," she smiled, "why don't you kiss the girl?"

Everyone went nuts, just as she'd planned. Clay didn't care, knowing that Laurel was in on it. Feeling lightheaded and in the arms of the boy she admired most, Greenlee didn't object when he leaned toward her and planted a great big kiss on her. What she didn't expect was his hand gently sliding up the back of her shirt, staying there too long, with all of the flashes going off like lightning. Everyone was laughing as they snapped pics and posted them as fast as they took them. Comments were hitting the TGP page as they stood there in the backyard. Even Clay couldn't have imagined he'd be this big of a hit.

Picture posted: Clay kissing Greenlee, hand up the back of her shirt.

A.J. – **First base?**

Griff – **Golden lays one on her and feels her up . . . kinda**

Tucker – **Golden getting lucky**
Quinton – **Greenlee's the go-to girl** ☺
Larry43 – **Golden's gonna get lucky**
A.J. – **TD if ya know what I mean**
Larry43 – **Who knew? Greenlee, that easy**
Griff – **He's going inside…**

Greenlee removed his arm and gave him a dirty look, but still followed him back into the house as he led her by the hand. Stumbling, she grabbed his arm, not realizing the full effects that the punch was having on her. Clearly it was kicking in, more so than she knew. Kids were everywhere, talking loudly, goofing around, laughing, and having fun. Problem was that most of it was at her expense, and she didn't have a clue.

Audrey and Marianne hadn't followed her; at the others' insistence, they'd stayed with Griff, Tucker, A.J., and Laurel. Clay looked over his shoulder at Greenlee; she smiled, and he smiled back at her. Clay mouthed, "Are you okay?"

"I think so. Yes. I'm okay." She moved closer to him and they continued to walk down the hallway.

Stumbling again, she tightened her grip around him. Clay pulled her closer, trying to stabilize her as she walked.

"Are you sure?" Clay asked her, certain she wasn't being completely truthful. He was right.

"Actually, Clay, I think I need to go home. I don't feel so good," she whispered. "Seriously, I'm starting to feel sick like earlier. I'm sorry. I don't feel good."

"You just need to lie down," Clay responded, placing his arms around her.

"No, I don't feel good. Can you find Marianne, please?"

He led her into an empty room, one of the boy's bedrooms. Turning on a lamp, he cleared off the bed and sat her down on the edge. Greenlee swept the hair that had fallen across her face to the side, pushed it behind her ears, and took massive deep breaths, hoping to calm herself. Her stomach wasn't cooperating and puking seemed inevitable. Horrified at the thought of spewing in front of Clay, she wanted to leave immediately. She asked him again. This time she insisted, her tone sharp. He knew that he had to find her friends.

"Clay, please find Marianne. I need to leave. I feel sick."

She flopped sideways onto the bed and, against his better judgment, he pulled out his phone and snapped a picture of her lying down with her hair scattered across her face. He took a deep breath and posted it.

Caption: *she wants more . . . okay!*

"Dude, I'll be right back. I'll find your friend."

Immediately comments hit the post.

Duckdog – **Give it to her hahahaha**
Larry43 – **That was easy**
Griff – **Brilliant idea – meeting**
A.J. – **See ya in 2**
Golden – **1**
Duckdog – **There**
Larry43 – **Can I**
A.J. – **No**
Golden – **Hahah . . . don't push it Larry** ☺
Larry43 – **Gotcha . . . NOT JK**
Tucker – **TGP's friends approaching**
Larry43 – **Got it**
A.J. – **Sweet**

Laurel approached Audrey and Marianne. "Will you help me find Brittany and Kelsey? What's your friend's name again, Greenlee?"

"Greenlee, yeah. Actually, have you seen her?"

"No I haven't. Marianne, isn't it?"

Marianne nodded but continued to look around the living room. Audrey whispered in her ear but it was too loud in the house and Marianne didn't hear a word that Audrey had said.

"We may as well join forces and look for them together. Come on. You help me, I'll help you, and then we'll all hang, deal?"

"Fine." Marianne nudged Audrey, "What she said," then burst out laughing.

Laurel grabbed both girls and redirected them away from the boy's room. Texting Kelsey for an assist, her words "*over here now idiot*" weren't received very well.

"Rude!"

"Seriously," Brittany agreed. "Who does she think she is, anyway?"

"Laurel!" Kelsey laughed. "That's who."

And there she was, Laurel, standing in front of them and grinning from ear to ear. Marianne and Audrey of all people were at her side. Brittany and Kelsey stopped dead in their tracks, glanced at each other and then back at the odd threesome. Odd didn't begin to describe Laurel hanging out with these two.

"Look, we have new friends," Laurel said with a giggle.

"Did you bump your head or what?" Kelsey added, "No offense."

"None taken. Weird, for us too, right?" Marianne responded.

"We really need to find Greenlee," Audrey insisted. "Marianne, let's keep looking."

Laurel's head spun toward Kelsey, her eyes narrowed to near perfect slits. Message delivered; time to shut up and go along with whatever Laurel was up too.

"Let's grab drinks and we'll look for her. She's here somewhere, " Kelsey said.

"Kelsey, that's the smartest thing you've said all evening." Pulling Marianne's sleeve toward her, Laurel added, "Grab the other girl, what's her name again? Oh yeah, Audrey. Let's go. The party's just getting started!"

Chapter 22 - Hurry up!

Duckdog stood guard outside the bedroom door. Over a dozen boys filled the room: A.J. Griff, Tucker, Quinton, Riley, Dakota, Colton, Hayden, and, of course, Clay. Clay nudged Greenlee. She stirred, sat up, tried to stand, but was too wobbly on her feet and sat back down. All the guys had their phones out. Greenlee reached out for Clay; he spoke softly and kindly to her. The boys in the background never said a word. Placing a cool washcloth on her head, he eased her back down on the bed, and though she objected, he pulled off her shoes. He insisted she'd feel much better if she rested. She sat back up and said she was thirsty and needed something to drink. He nodded. *She must be dehydrated,* he thought.

"I'll get you something," he said. "But then you really need to sleep this off for a while."

He looked around the room, trying not to laugh, and one of the guys handed him a cup. Clay stared into the bottom of it, but A.J. motioned toward Greenlee. He shook his head no and then went off to the bathroom and pretended to puke, went to the sink, and refilled the cup with water. Walking back into the room, he sat on the edge of the bed and handed her the cup.

"Sip it slowly, tiny sips, you know what I mean?"

She didn't answer. Greenlee sipped the water.

"You'll feel better in a bit," he reassured her. "But you really do need to rest."

Greenlee stared at him as he spoke, but she was having trouble focusing. His face was a blur. She continued to sip. Not being able to define the taste of the contents of the cup anymore, she took one last sip and tried to hand the cup back to him. It slipped out of her hand and fell to the floor, splashing water on the bedspread, carpet, and Clay. Greenlee hadn't even noticed that she'd missed his hand. Her head was spinning and nausea had overcome her. It was the oddest combination of hot, clammy, and dizzy, a feeling that she'd never experienced before. Clay grabbed the washcloth and reapplied it to her forehead. The boys tried to contain their laughter, but they got louder and louder. Clay raised his hands in an attempt to quiet them down, but it wasn't working. It didn't matter anyway. Greenlee was long gone, passed out, oblivious to everything around her.

"Dude, she's out!" Tucker announced, stating the obvious.

Greenlee's limp body lay curled up on the bed. She lay motionless, almost greenish in color. Ironic. *She turned the color of her name, Greenlee*, Clay thought to himself.

"Hurry up: let's do this, fake it for the pics."

"Hang on a sec, A.J." Clay grabbed Tucker's arm as he moved toward the bed. Tucker stopped and waited for A.J.'s okay to move.

"Dude, come on Golden, we gotta move now. Why are you still standing there? It's not real, dude! It's part of the game."

The only thing between Greenlee and a dozen boys, the rest of the secret initiation, was Clay. For a second he had a moment of doubt. Was this going too far? He pushed the thought out of his head. He was almost done. It was almost over. He could be with Laurel. He'd go down as pulling off the greatest initiation ever, his own, and then could go back to doing what he loved, playing football. *Just do it*, he told himself. He pulled out his phone and placed his finger on top of the record button. Video was rolling.

"Seriously dude, come on," A.J. placed his hand on Clay's shoulder and noticed his phone was recording. "Good boy!"

"This has to stay on The Greenlee Project page, that's all, you know what I mean? I'm going finish this, but just saying . . . that's all!"

A.J. nodded, squeezed Clay's shoulder, stepped back, made eye contact with every boy in the room, and made an announcement.

"Golden has my word, our word, that this is still a secret. This initiation will go down in history. There is too much at stake. This stays only on the TGP page."

Everyone agreed.

"Let's do this!"

The boys placed Greenlee in a suggestive position on the bed. Clay lay next to her, leaned over, and they placed her arm and her legs over him. They pulled her shirt out of her jeans, and he placed one of his hands up the front of it. Other boys took pictures with her, too. Greenlee had no idea, and albeit the boys knowingly faked each scene, they didn't think twice about what they were doing. It was as if they'd momentarily forgotten who they were supposed to be; lost in the moment, the boys posted the terrible pics.

Pic: Greenlee in a suggestive photo. Caption: ***Greenlee—the go-to girl!***

Tucker – **Golden, touchdown!**
A.J. – **That didn't take long**
Duckdog – **Next**
Griff – **Golden IS golden**
Colton – **Nice**
Larry43 – **Dude really, that easy**
Clay – **Still not what you think, but yeah**
Larry43 – **Gotcha**
Hayden – **My hero**
Quincy – **Score**

"Let's do one more for the page, last one," Tucker suggested. "This is bad."

He was laughing so hard that Greenlee stirred. A.J. punched him playfully in the arm, and he whispered his suggestion. Clay's conscience, not on his side, was overwrought with spiked punch and egged on by the laughter, chuckles, and cheers. Knowing that he'd scored the respect of every dude on the entire team, A.J. included, the final blow was truly awful. One by one the boys crawled onto the bed and posed with Greenlee, all at the same time. They posted it immediately. Greenlee, in a comatose state, had no idea that they were surrounding her. They posed her in humiliating and suggestive positions and climbed all over her.

"We gotta go, now, before we're missed out there," Clay stated. "Hey, do you think she's okay? I mean, should we call someone?"

Duckdog leaned over her mouth and checked her vital signs. "She's breathing. Let's tell her friends to take her home."

"Dude get the cloth, wet it again, and we'll all get the hell out of here. Find one of her friends and tell them to look for her, you know what I mean? Let them find her like this."

A.J. was right. Clay didn't need to be anywhere near Greenlee when her friends found her in this state. The boys straightened Greenlee out into a normal position. She mumbled, asking for Marianne. They didn't answer her, but her voice brought them a little relief: it would appear that she was coming back around.

Clay walked with his friends back through the house. They were laughing at each other's posts, commenting and joking. Hits and likes were adding up, and the group seemed larger than it had been earlier that night.

"How did this group get so big?" Clay asked. "I thought it was just for the team? It seems massive now."

"Well it was supposed to be just the team, but it's complicated," A.J. said with a laugh. "Relax, dude, if they're in the group, then they're supposed to be. They were added or approved by me, you, Tuck, or Griff."

Clay nodded his head. "Just got big, that's all."

Laurel sneaked up behind him and whispered in his ear, "Nice job, Golden, I'm impressed."

She snickered as she pointed to one of the latest posts. Clay blushed, knowing that he didn't feel anything for Greenlee.

Laurel's big green eyes were sparkling. She was pleased, very pleased, indeed, with the dose of humiliation they had handed to Greenlee. He leaned toward her and quickly pecked her on the cheek. She stepped back quickly and motioned toward Marianne and Audrey.

"Ah, just the girls I needed to see," he winked at Laurel. "Hey! Have you girls seen Greenlee? I can't find her anywhere." Marianne looked stunned. "We thought she was with you! We were about to ask you the same thing. Where the hell is she, then?"

"No, dude, she was. But then she didn't feel good and went looking for you. I told her I'd help find you, but I couldn't, till now. Now you're here, and I can't find Greenlee." He paused and glanced at Audrey. "Have you seen her?"

"No, stupid. Sorry, I'm just worried." She looked down the hallway. "We'd better find her, though, it's getting late and we're going to be busted if we don't leave now!"

Clay hollered across the room, "Hey A.J.! Have you seen Greenlee?"

A.J. shook his head. "No, dude. Sorry."

"Well let's find her then, no worries," Clay suggested. "Split up and we'll all look."

Marianne was the first to find her. She was perched on the edge of the bed, literally green, her hair stuck to her forehead, and trembling.

"Oh my God, you look like crap! Are you okay?"

Marianne ran to her side and put her arm around her shoulder. Greenlee didn't speak, but shook her head. Audrey grabbed the washcloth and wet it again, placing it gently on Greenlee's forehead. She looked around the room for Greenlee's shoes. Greenlee looked like she was about to puke.

"We've gotta get her out of here. Is your sister here?" asked Audrey.

Marianne nodded, though she had no idea how they'd get Greenlee home without her puking in her sister's car. Greenlee gingerly rose to her feet. She put her arm around Marianne, but to her surprise, Clay suddenly put his arm around her waist.

"I've gotcha," he said. "Here, lean on me."

He smiled at her, and she even managed a faint, fragile smile back.

"I think that punch may have had quite a kick, huh?" he said sincerely. "Don't answer that, I already know."

"I'm so sorry," she whispered, "I really don't know what hit me, but it did. It just hit me."

"Don't worry about it. I just want you to feel better, okay?"

He helped walk her out to the car and Marianne even thanked him for being so sweet. Marianne's sister rolled her eyes, opened the window, and insisted that Greenlee hang her head out of the window on the way home.

"I'm not cleaning puke out of my car. Get in and don't look down. Take deep breaths and you'll be fine in the morning. Trust me." She handed her a plastic bag. "If you need this, use it. You will feel better tomorrow, I promise, but don't ever do that again!"

Greenlee nodded, too weak to object. She placed her hands on top of the opened window and rested her chin on her hands. She didn't dare close her eyes for fear of her stomach emptying out. Her mind drifted to Clay's beautiful smile. His words raced through her head, especially the line where he'd told her he thought that she was cute. She could still feel his touch as he pulled her toward him, and still remember his face when he leaned in and kissed her. As horrible as she felt, she'd still had a wonderful evening. The boy who'd captivated her, who had invited her to a party, had taken the time to compliment her, taken care of her and made her smile. He'd kissed her and had taken the time to walk her to the car and send her off. *What a sweetheart*, she thought. Greenlee couldn't believe that, despite how bad she felt, this evening could possibly rank as one of the greatest nights of her life!

Chapter 23 - Malice in Action

Marianne held Greenlee's hair as she puked nonstop. Audrey flushed, mopped her friend's brow, and stayed on the lookout for her mom. Feeling as if her insides were on fire, her head about to explode and her sides aching from the constant retching, Greenlee thought that she might possibly die.

"Do you think we should call someone?" Audrey asked, scared for her friend. "Do you think she's okay?"

Marianne shook her head. "Don't call anybody. I think she's over the worst of it. My sister said this part is the worst, but if she could sip some water or soda, that might help."

Audrey ran down the stairs into the kitchen and poured a soda over ice, grabbed a few crackers, and ran back up the stairs three at a time. Marianne had helped Greenlee back to the bed. She was at least able to lie down now without puking, which the girls viewed as a great sign. Helping her sit up, Marianne had Greenlee sip the cold liquid. It burned her throat, but she managed to hold it down. Declining the crackers, she rested her face against the cool pillow.

"I'm so stupid," she said rubbing her eyes and pushing her hair behind her ears. Greenlee looked at her friends, who had taken such great care of her. "I just can't believe that punch went down so easy and came back so bad. Ewwww."

All three of them giggled.

"Trust me, I will never, ever, ever do that again! Lesson learned."

Marianne handed her the soda and Greenlee managed another sip. She felt weak and tired, but she wanted to talk about Clay. She sat up and leaned against the headboard.

"Did you see him, I mean, before we left?"

"Don't you remember?" Marianne asked. "He walked you to the car."

"I don't remember all of it, but I thought that he did. Isn't that awful, that I can't remember?"

"Well, don't beat yourself up too badly. But you're right: none of us can do this again. It was stupid. We could have been suffering from alcohol poisoning."

Greenlee squeezed Audrey's hand. "Thank you. I know I don't deserve such good friends. Thank you both for taking care of me tonight. I swear, I thought I was dying!"

"We thought you were dying. You scared us to death!" Marianne said as she rolled her eyes and flopped down next to Greenlee. "Seriously, we almost called your mom."

"Seriously?"

"Yes, Greenlee, seriously!"

Audrey nodded. "We were scared. You were in bad shape and to be honest, we weren't really sure what we had been drinking." She lay across the foot of the bed and smiled. "You know, we were all stupid. Did you hear what I said? We didn't know what we were drinking! How dumb is that, for real?"

"Well, enough of that! We all learned our lessons. I say that we make a pact and agree that we never do that again, any of us."

Greenlee raised her hand. "Agreed!"

Audrey stuck her hand out too. "Right!"

"So, Greenlee, what happened with Clay?" Marianne asked with a grin.

* * *

Laurel couldn't stand waiting. She kept checking her phone as she read the posts and added comments without Brittany and Kelsey noticing. It didn't work. At times she laughed out loud and it drew more attention to her. Even her BFF asked what on earth she was reading.

"It's that funny? If it's that good, then share it," said Brittany.

Still laughing, Laurel tapped her phone. "I can't, seriously, it's a private joke."

Brittany glanced over Laurel's shoulder; Laurel covered her phone with her hand. She continued to text as her friends tried to look on.

"Seriously . . . come on!" Brittany snapped playfully. "You can't tell us?"

"What's up with that anyway? Your new BFF?" Kelsey chimed in.

Grabbing Laurel's phone, Brittany playfully threw it to Kelsey. The girls passed it back and forth between each other so many times it finally timed out.

"Ha! Password protected," Laurel said with a laugh. "Give me my phone back, dorks."

Brittany tossed the phone back to Laurel. Ticked off, she scolded her. "Really . . . we're your friends and you won't tell us what's going on? Seriously, Laurel?"

"I'm not going to tell you," Laurel replied wickedly. "I'm going to show you."

She had a devious smile unlike any that they'd seen before. This was new. Laurel shook her head and pointed toward her brother in the driver's seat, and the girls realized it was merely a matter of time before she filled them in. It must be big! Laurel was excited and so secretive. What had she done?

"Here . . . get out . . . just kidding, love ya, sis!"

"Thank you, bro. Love you too, loser!"

The girls piled onto Laurel's bed. She grabbed her laptop and immediately pulled up *The Greenlee Project* page. Hardly being able to contain herself, Laurel turned to the girls. Her face had an odd, almost malicious look.

"You have to swear not to tell a single person about what I'm about to show you. This is private, so swear it!"

Kelsey tried to peer over the laptop. "Come on already, give. What is this?"

"Swear it!"

Laurel started laughing and gave the girls the backstory of *The Greenlee Project* and the web page. Her friends were shocked as they tried to grasp the concept of what she said. Was she serious? This didn't make sense.

"Girl, I think you had too much punch."

"Yeah, what she said," Kelsey agreed, stunned at what she'd just heard.

Barely containing her laughter, Laurel repeated one more time the story behind TGP and Clay's initiation for the football team. That Greenlee was the *project*, and how Clay had pretended to like her. How the party had been a setup, complete with the punch, the pictures, and all of the posts.

"Don't you get it?" Laurel asked. "It's all one big joke."

She turned the laptop around for them to view the page for themselves, revealing the posts from the very beginning. All the conversations, the walks down the hall, even when he'd kicked her chair in class. All of this had been recorded through text messages, photos, and video. All of it was right there, including the horrific pictures from the bedroom.

"OMG, look at that one! Is that real? It looks real," Kelsey squealed.

"I know, right? It looks like she's been making out with all of them, and other stuff."

Laurel continued to scroll through the pictures and posts. "That's me. Larry43. Look what I wrote. It's so funny!"

The girls read the posts and laughed. They commented on the comments that other people had made and interacted with the guys who were online, commenting as Larry43.

"This is too funny," Kelsey said as she grabbed her phone. "We have to share this with Taylor, she'd get such a kick out of this, and she's having that swim party next week with the upperclassmen. This would guarantee our invite!"

"She's right," Brittany agreed. "It's your call, Laurel, but I think we should share it. Look at that one: Greenlee can't even stand up!"

"Taylor's a junior and super popular. Everyone's going to that party. Let's send it in a private message and she can forward it if she wants to, cause I'm guessing she will," Laurel laughed.

"Oh yeah," the girls said in unison.

The message: *Hey thought you'd get a kick out of this, so funny, right? Haha! What an idiot!*

The damage was done. Taylor opened the message, laughed out loud, passed the phone around, hit forward, and sent it to everyone she knew. But it wasn't just the girls who were breaking the rules regarding the secrecy of the group. Leaks were being made on both sides of the fence. No one even knew which kid at the party, girl or guy, had forwarded it on to the "guru" who had mad skills and turned each individual post into one long video. The movie was hilarious at first, but then it became humiliating. It was obscene and it had been posted for the entire world to see on *You've got footage, post here!*—a popular website for videos. Once posted, the shares had gone through the roof. Even Larry43 couldn't resist forwarding and posting the footage. Rolling on the floor, laughing till they cried, the girls, the kids at the party, half of the school, most of whom Greenlee didn't know, had watched her make a fool of herself and appear in many provocative scenarios that she had no memory of. The kids were passing and sharing the video as if it were the next best thing. Horrified, Clay picked up his phone.

Clay – **Dude, what the hell!**
A.J. – **Man . . . don't know**
Clay – **What do we do?**
A.J. – **Sit tight**
Clay – **Who did it?**
A.J. – **Dunno**
Clay – **This is bad**
A.J. – **Ya think, yeah**

Clay – **How do we get it down?**
A.J. – **Working on it**
Clay – **I'm freaking!**
A.J. – **Tell me about it**
Quincy – **Dude, it's viral!**

Laurel's text from Clay wasn't exactly the one she'd hoped for, but she was happy to receive it anyway. He asked if she knew anything about the video, which technically she didn't, so she naturally denied having anything to do with spreading it. She assured him that she would try to track down her brother because he might be able to help them remove it from the site. *Try to relax,* she told him. Clay couldn't possibly relax now. He watched the video again. What were they thinking? It appeared a million times worse than what had actually happened, and that was bad enough! He knew that! But at least the things that were suggested in the video hadn't actually happened and Greenlee didn't have a clue! Clay thought to himself that his freaking life was over!

Sitting on his floor, sick to his stomach, he watched the video receive hit after hit after hit. The color slipped from his face just as his mother knocked on his door.

"Son, I'm going to bed now. Do you need anything?" she asked as she opened his bedroom door a crack.

He shook his head. He tried to respond, but he had a frog in his throat. He cleared it, and tried to speak again. "No, Mom, I'm good."

"You look tired, son, are you okay?"

He nodded.

"Okay, get some rest."

He tried to smile, but he knew that she saw right through him. He fought for control of his emotions. Shaking, he realized how much trouble all of them were about to be in. With the phone still in his hands, he started texting every teammate he could think of that may have computer skills, or family members with skills. He had to get that video off the page now. Despite all of his hard work, his studies, the football camps, and his best efforts, he would still disappoint his dad. He thought of all of the coaches, his mom, and the rest of his family. It had all gone down the drain for a stupid initiation.

What about Greenlee? Had she seen it yet? She was a real person who would be seriously affected by what he'd done. He pushed her out of his mind and focused on trying to fix the biggest problem that he perceived: the video and how to remove it.

Clay – **Dude, can you fix it?**
Duckdog – **It's funny, did you 'like' it. JK**
Duckdog – **Definitely gotta come down**
Duckdog – **Looking for someone right now**
Clay – **Who did it?**
Duckdog – **Dunno? U**
Clay – **Dunno**
Duckdog – **Colton's brother, real techie. He could help**
Clay – **check it out**
Duckdog – **K**
Clay – **Could kill who did this**
Duckdog – **Right!**

Clay was pacing the floor, making one call after another, while he monitored the video. Every kid in school had to have seen it by now, he'd bet on it. And since it had gone viral, they were dead, all of them. They'd never play ball again, and forget any chance of getting a scholarship or being accepted into a decent school. They had to remove the evidence, the video, all of it—now. We've gotta take down the page! Clay sent a group message.

Clay – **Delete the page! Now. TGP**
A.J. – **Good idea!!!!!!!!!!! Do it!!!!!!!**
Colton – **I'll do it, takes 14 days to take effect**
Clay – **Seriously????**
Colton – **Yep, deleted one before**
A.J. – **It will stop people from posting though, right?**

Colton – **Yes, no new posts!**
Clay – **Maybe we can delete posts or something?**
Colton – **I'll check it out**
Clay – **Thnx**

It was safe to say that Clay didn't sleep that night—none of the boys did. All of them saw pending consequences for their actions running through their minds. They would be severe, without question, and likely from more than once source: school, parents, and maybe even the authorities. They were all in serious trouble, and they knew it. Colton had deleted the TGP page, but as he'd said, it would take time to pull the page down. No new posts could be added, but unfortunately old posts couldn't be deleted either. For the next two weeks people could still read the posts, listen to recorded conversations, and, to everyone's horror, because someone had posted the link to the infamous video, watch that, too.

Clay panicked. He stood motionless outside his parents' room. He could hear his dad snoring. He opened the door and stepped into their room. Watching them sleep, knowing the disappointment that he would cause them, he backed out again. Maybe, just maybe, they could fix it on their own. He was doubtful, but he had hope.

Greenlee was sound asleep and didn't have a clue what had gone down. Her friends were asleep beside her, one next to her, one on the floor. Her last thought before she slipped off to sleep was of Clay. His beautiful smile and dark brown eyes made her smile. She reflected on his touch as he gently whispered in her ear. The way he moved closer to her and slid his arm in the arch of her back. She could still hear his voice when he asked her to step outside.

"Let's go talk," he'd said. "I like you, and you're kinda hot."

She remembered him telling her to wait right there, him handing her a drink and helping her down. She remembered him getting a cold rag, looking for Marianne, taking off her shoes. She didn't know why sleep came so easy with such pleasant thoughts. Clay was on her mind and she thought it was a lovely way to fall asleep. Greenlee couldn't wait to go to school the next day. She was dying to hear from him.

Chapter 24 – Laughingstock

"You're going to be late! Come on already, Greenlee. You're going to make me late!"

In the kitchen, Matt Granger topped off another cup of coffee. "What does she do up there? How long does it take to throw on a pair of jeans, t-shirt, and shoes?" He stormed to the bottom of the stairs and hollered again. "Greenlee, come on!"

Mrs. Granger continued emptying the dishwasher. Her voice was calm. "She's in high school now, and she's going to take a little longer in the mornings to get ready."

She could tell that her husband had waited long enough, regardless of Greenlee's carefree attitude. He still had to be at work at a certain time. Grabbing his keys, coffee, and kissing his wife on the cheek, he walked toward the door.

"Tell her I'm in the car. She's got one minute."

Before he could leave, Greenlee came flying down the stairs, grabbed a piece of fruit, hugged her mom, and ran out the door. Her face was beaming and her mom knew immediately there was something going on.

"Gotta go."

"Hey!" her dad complained.

"What?"

"I'm going be late. You need to get up earlier if you're going to take longer in the mornings to get ready. By the way, don't wear so much eyeliner, please."

Panicking, Greenlee asked, "Do I look okay?"

"You just don't need that much makeup, your eyes are perfect already. Greenlee, you're beautiful!"

Greenlee kissed her mom, smiled, and left. Her dad backed out of the driveway before the car door was even shut and Greenlee's seat belt fastened. He wasn't happy and she knew it: likely a good time to apologize.

"I'm sorry, Dad. I'll get up earlier tomorrow, promise."

He glanced at her, looked back at the road, only to look again at the daughter who sat beside him. *When had she grown up?* he wondered. She smiled at him, and he couldn't help but think how pretty she looked.

"You like nice," he commented as he drove.

"Thanks."

"Why?"

"Why what?" She laughed.

"Why are you all made up?"

Greenlee giggled. "I didn't think that I was! I'm really not."

"I guess not. Must be me. I blinked and you grew up. Wow. I guess you really are growing up." He drove a few minutes. "I really would appreciate it if you did get up a tad earlier. I hate feeling so rushed. I prefer the drive in to work to be relaxing and uneventful, if you don't mind."

"No problem."

"Thank you."

Marianne sent a text as soon as she was dropped at the curb. Greenlee replied: **almost there**. Audrey pulled up behind Greenlee.

"Do I look okay?" Greenlee asked her.

"You look great, really. Love the shirt," Marianne said, pointing at the ruffled sheer top that Greenlee had chosen. "The tank underneath it is a different color. Perfect touch."

Audrey was all smiles.

"Don't mind her," Marianne grinned. "She's on the lookout. "That dude, what's his name?"

"Quinton," Audrey answered, still scoping out the kids walking into the school.

"Yeah, that dude texted her. He said that he'd had fun hanging out with her, wanted to hang at school."

As they walked along their regular route, they noticed that something wasn't quite right. All the kids around them were having discussions and staring at them. A few of them even pointed. Marianne, Audrey, and Greenlee had no idea what was going on. Greenlee's hair had been straightened. She wore makeup and had paired it with a carefully chosen outfit, all in the hopes of looking just right in order to catch the eye of the guy who had captivated her.

The TGP page, the videos, conversations, links, all had made their way through entire the school and just about everybody who was anybody had seen something from the page. The video had received thousands of hits. Little Greenlee wasn't so innocent any more. Overnight she'd become the class laughingstock, the biggest joke ever pulled. Her reputation was ruined and the day hadn't even started yet.

Greenlee was oblivious to the fact that everyone was staring and laughing at her, but she picked up that something was wrong. The whispering and the laughing were obvious and suddenly she felt nervous and insecure.

Greenlee whispered to her friends, "What's going on?"

They shrugged their shoulders, not knowing themselves what was happening. Clay walked around the corner and Greenlee's face lit up, but her heart sank as soon as he looked away and pretended that he didn't know her. Her friends watched Greenlee try to hide her embarrassment. Batting back tears that had formed in her eyes, she dug into her purse. Clay hadn't slept since he first viewed the video. Horrified at the thought of what was about to happen, he couldn't face her. Hell, it was a struggle looking at himself.

Marianne squeezed her friend's hand and whispered that everything would be okay. Greenlee nodded, but didn't say a word. She wasn't prepared for the person she bumped into next, Laurel.

"Well, hello Greenlee, superstar."

Laurel had a smirk on her face that Greenlee couldn't identify and she had no idea what she was talking about. Clearly Laurel had an agenda. Greenlee's instincts about her were right, as Laurel fired off another bizarre question.

"So remember that party at Duckdog's? Where did you and Clay disappear to?" She snickered and added, "And all of the other guys, if you know what I mean?"

"No, Laurel, I don't know what you mean," snapped Greenlee.

"Interesting," she said, flipping her hair and waltzing off in another direction. Brittany and Kelsey looked Greenlee up and down.

"What's that all about?" Marianne asked. "The wicked witch is back! There must be flying monkeys around here somewhere."

Greenlee actually smiled. "She is a witch!"

"I don't like her. What were we thinking, talking to her that night, anyway? It must have been the punch!"

Greenlee entered her first-period class and sat down in her regular seat. A paper with the letters *TGP* was stuck to the back of it. Marianne leaned forward and pulled it off, not knowing what it was. The girls merely trashed it without paying attention to the meaning. Griff covered his mouth and faked a cough of "TGP."

Stares, finger-pointing, and ugly remarks were now becoming painfully obvious to Greenlee, too obvious to ignore. She knew without a doubt that she was the topic of whatever was going on. Reaching into her backpack, she texted Marianne and Audrey.

Greenlee – **What the hell?**

Marianne – **Dunno, about to find out**

Audrey – **Betting Laurel has something do with whatever's going on**

Greenlee – **True**

Marianne – **Wait a few minutes, we'll find out**

Greenlee – **K**

Marianne's head hung over her desk, her ears attentive to the conversations around her. Greenlee did the same, listening to the conversations others were having in the room. Gasps followed by giggles came from the corner of the room. Derogatory comments followed that, and if Greenlee wasn't mistaken, her name was mentioned. Her face began to flush. Her heart raced as she realized that she was in the midst of something, but didn't know what it was. Her eyes still directed down, she looked to her left and waited for Audrey to glance her way. Audrey didn't offer comfort, only concern, as she too tried to figure out the details of the situation. One thing was for sure: Greenlee's name kept popping up.

"Dude, that's hilarious!"

"Can you believe it, who knew?"

"Did you think she'd do that?"

The next comment gutted her: "Golden is pure gold." Greenlee knew all too well that Clay was often referred to as *Golden,* a nickname that he'd received on day one. Laurel's voice filled the room as she purposely spoke loudly. Her comments pierced Greenlee's ears as Clay sat silently.

"Did you have any idea that was her?" and "Did you see it?"

What were they looking at? Panicked, Greenlee turned around and looked at Marianne. Her eyes were huge and her face was filled with worry. She motioned toward the corner with her eyes. Marianne peered in that direction just as they all turned and looked away. Awkward whispers and giggles were hushed by the teacher. Class started and phones were put away, but Greenlee's nerves were on edge and rightfully so. Her gut instincts were right: something was majorly wrong.

Clay sat in the back of the room next to Griff, Tucker, and A.J., who all acted as if they had no idea what was going on. Clay didn't dare glance her way; it was as if she didn't even exist. From putting on the hot and heavy on Friday night, to giving her the coldest shoulder she'd ever experienced, Greenlee didn't understand what he was doing. She knew the others were laughing at her, but she didn't know why. Unable to able to handle the ridicule anymore, Greenlee stood up, excused herself, and went to the ladies' room. Splashing cold water on her face, she texted her mom.

Greenlee – **Don't feel good. Can I come home?**
Mrs. Granger – **Hang in there**

Finding an empty stall, she allowed the tears to flow down her cheeks. If she'd only known what was about to unfold she may have been able to prepare for it. The impact had already started to hit, but the magnitude of the damage had yet to surface. She could feel it all around her: she'd done something wrong. Heart heavy and nerves shot, she stepped out of the stall, washed her face, reapplied her makeup as best as she could, and walked back to class. When she sat back down at her desk, there it was again. A sign taped to her chair: TGP. This time, the words *get you some Golden*, had been added. Greenlee knew immediately that whatever it was had something to do with Clay. She couldn't breathe. Dying to cry and daring herself not to, she took the deepest breath she could in order to delay the tears that had formed in her eyes. Something was going down and unfortunately she was smack in the middle of it.

"Slut."

Greenlee's head shot up. WTH! Surely that comment wasn't meant for her! She had no idea who'd said the terrible word. As soon as the bell rang, the girls gathered in the hallway. Marianne held up her phone.

"I've got something to show you." She looked concerned. "Greenlee, it's bad."

She didn't have a chance to share it with her friend. Greenlee's phone vibrated in her hand. She didn't recognize the number but she did recognize the letters. *TGP*. Staring at the number, she tried to figure out what the letters stood for, but she couldn't. Another text came in, same number, same letters, TGP, but this time a link had been included. Greenlee hit the link and stared in horror as *The Greenlee Project* page popped up. Her picture was the profile pic. Recreational hunting 4x4 was the background. Reading post after post, which included every challenge that Clay had accepted regarding her, she covered her mouth with her hand and gasped aloud when she saw the attached audio files. Clicking on them, she realized that it was several of the conversations that she'd had with Clay! What a freaking JERK!

There were pictures, lots of pictures, that she hadn't known had been taken. Naturally, they were awful, unflattering and unkind, to say the least; scrolling down as fast as she could, she finally came to the link of the video. She stood between Marianne and Audrey. All were mortified at the images before them.

"OMG, freaking loser!"

"I just can't believe it, Marianne! How didn't we know?"

Greenlee looked over her shoulder and stared down the guy she had thought had liked her *for real*. In that moment, he knew she knew. He turned around as if she was nothing. She didn't dare glance at his friends, knowing with one look she'd surely lose it. Her hands were shaking, her chest heaving. She didn't dare move for fear of falling or bursting into tears.

"Do you want to watch this now? Here?"

"Click it, Marianne. I don't think I can."

Marianne clicked the link and the three girls watched as Greenlee made a fool of herself, drinking the punch as if it were soda and watching the boys create challenges and posting them while she did not realize what they were doing. Clay was even hanging all over Laurel at one point, kissing her in a corner. Greenlee stumbling and hanging on Clay as he snapped more pics, but so did everyone else. The final blow, the dreaded bedroom scene, was beyond horrific. It was more humiliating than anyone could or should endure. This was an obvious setup. Clearly she was out of it, but the scenes didn't really depict that. They'd done a good job, splicing the videos together to appear as if the scenes were something else entirely. *The Greenlee Project.* She had truly been Golden's biggest personal achievement.

The boy she thought had taken such good care of her had set her up and humiliated her. He knew that none of these things had happened—even in the terrible state she'd been in that night, she knew it, he knew it, and every one of those kids at the party had known it. No wonder people were laughing at her. How many people had seen the video? She clicked the link again just to be sure it had come from the site she'd thought it had. Unfortunately it had, the hits now reaching the thousands. OMG! Her parents! Why? Why had this happened? Why had this happened *to her*? Why had this freaking loser picked *her*? What had she done to deserve this? Greenlee, despite her friends' objections, turned and simply walked away. Marianne and Audrey started to follow, but a teacher's voice yelled and stopped them in their tracks. Turning around, they walked into lab.

Marianne – **OMG Greenlee, get back here**
Audrey – **Greenlee, answer ur text**
Marianne – **Greenlee, it's important**

As soon as the bell rang, Clay left as fast as he could. Everyone was congratulating him, but he couldn't stop to talk. His head hung low, avoiding eye contact, feeling suddenly ashamed. He wasn't proud of what he'd done. He had no idea that the video had been made, let alone gone viral. Even football wasn't on his mind, but Greenlee was. It occurred to him that if this had happened to his sister, he would be furious with the guys who'd done it. He'd kick their butts, he thought. He didn't know what to do. He wasn't proud of what they'd, no, *he'd* done. He'd give anything to take it back. Clay climbed in his truck and left the campus.

Greenlee's tears were streaming down her face, inconsolable. She had walked to the nurse's office. Jumping to her feet, the nurse asked her what was wrong. Greenlee couldn't talk. She could barely breathe. Handing her a tissue, the nurse blotted her face dry.

"What on earth is wrong?" the nurse asked. "Clearly, you're not okay."

"I don't feel very well," she replied, though not convincingly.

The nurse stared at her, needing more, but Greenlee sat listlessly on the chair as the nurse continued to ask her questions.

"What's wrong with you, dear? Let's take your temperature. How long have you felt this way?"

Getting nowhere, she placed a call to Greenlee's mom. To Greenlee's relief, she was being sent home. The conversation in the car was painful. Greenlee could hardly breathe, let alone talk; she cried the entire drive home.

"You're scaring me, Greenlee. What's going on?" Reaching over, her mom grabbed her hand. "You can tell me. You can tell me anything, you know that."

Greenlee tried to speak, but the crying had turned into sobbing. There was no way that she could tell her mom what was going on. Her tears rolled nonstop one after the other, all the way down her chin, and dripped onto her lap.

"Should I call Dad?" her mom asked, but Greenlee shook her head.

"Okay," her mom said softly. "Just relax, baby, we can talk about it in a minute, but you have to relax and you have to tell me what's going on."

Greenlee went straight to her room, flopped down on the bed, and sobbed into her pillow. Her mom sat next to her, talked soothingly, and rubbed her back, but it didn't seem to help. She texted Marianne, but Marianne didn't answer. Mrs. Granger couldn't decide if it was because she didn't want to share what was wrong with Greenlee or because she was in class. She chose to believe the latter.

"I'm going to fix you some tea," she said. Her daughter didn't answer. "Greenlee, did you hear me? I'm going to make you some tea. We'll have a cup, and then we will talk about whatever's going on, all right?"

Greenlee still didn't answer. Her mother stood up, kissed her daughter on the top of her head, and left the room. Texting the words **something upsetting Greenlee, call if you can**, she tried to reach her husband. He was clearly unavailable at the time. She placed a call, left a message, hung up, and as soon as she did the phone rang.

"Hey it's me, we have a situation. Sal, it's not good." Mrs. Granger listened as her friend spoke softly on the other end of the phone. "You'd better sit down, Sal. Really, it's going be a shock."

Speechless, Mrs. Granger listened to her friend Anne, Marianne's mother. The color washed from her face and she noticed that she was trembling. Trying to comprehend the words her friend was saying to her, she interrupted her.

"I'm sorry. Please slow down. Anne, say it again, please?"

Pacing the floor, her voice kept getting higher as she asked her friend the dreaded question, "Anne, what are you talking about? What is *The Greenlee Project?*"

To her horror she turned around and her beautiful, suddenly frail daughter stood at the door. She'd heard the words and knew her mother was about to find out the truth.

"Mom . . . Mom, no!" Greenlee begged.

Greenlee turned around and ran up the stairs. Her mother didn't even say goodbye to Anne. She dropped the phone, screamed Greenlee's name, and chased after her as fast as she could. She couldn't reach her in time. The bathroom door slammed before she got there, followed by the clicking of the lock.

Sally Granger sank down onto her knees, banged on the door, and begged her daughter to open it. Knowing something horrible had gone down, but not having an idea of the magnitude of what had happened to her girl, she tried one more time to discuss the situation with her daughter, but to no avail. Greenlee wasn't opening the door. Her eyes darted toward the stairs. Anne might still be on the line, though doubtful, she thought. She could call her back or beg Marianne, her daughter, to tell her. The things that she'd heard, she couldn't comprehend; surely, Greenlee couldn't possibly be *The Greenlee Project.*

"Greenlee, please I'm begging you, open the door. You know I can get in there if I need to, and right now I do, but I'd rather you open it on your own." She waited, but Greenlee didn't answer. She could hear her crying, sobbing, but saying nothing. She tried again to reason with her. "Whatever this is, Greenlee, whatever happened, we can figure it out together." No response. "Greenlee, whatever this is, you're not alone." There was still no answer.

"Greenlee, sweetheart, we can't help you if we don't know what it is. Baby, you have to tell us . . . what in the hell is *The Greenlee Project?*"

Greenlee would have given anything to be sound asleep, lost in exhaustion, rather than explain that she, of all things, was *The Greenlee Project.* Why did her mom answer the phone? Why did this happen at all?

Chapter 25 - Action

Clay drove around all day. He didn't answer his phone or his texts. His parents were concerned and his friends were out looking for him. The coaches were ticked off. Since the video had gone viral, the trouble they were in couldn't be undone, but none of that was on his mind. The look on Greenlee's face haunted him.

She'd suddenly appeared so wounded, so fragile. Like a real person; how stupid did that sound! *She* is *a real person*, he thought. He drove until his tank was almost dry, stopped for gas, and then kept driving. Contemplating calling his dad, he couldn't face the disappointment he caused. How did a joke, this initiation, go so wrong? He didn't mean for *The Greenlee Project* to end up as a public event. It was supposed to be a bit of fun with the team. He knew that what he'd done was wrong. Laurel texted him, but he didn't reply. He wasn't in the mood to talk even to her. His mom called, but he didn't answer. It went to voice mail. His dad called. Clay still didn't answer: voice mail again. The hole he'd dug was getting deeper and he didn't know where to go. Call after call kept coming in, text after text, and against his will he finally called home.

"Dad."

"Clay, get your butt home now, son, we need to talk."

"I can't, Dad. I can't come home just yet."

"Oh, yes you can, son! I think you're in enough trouble, don't you?"

Dead silence.

"Son, this is serious; this is a very serious matter. Come home now!" Pause. "Let's be clear, this is not a request."

There was still no reply. Wes Monning changed his approach.

"I'm pleading with you, son, we can work this out together, but you've got to come home."

"Dad, I can't, not yet."

"Son, you've got two seconds to make the right decision or I'm calling 911 and reporting your truck stolen." His dad's heart sank and Marjorie Monning jumped to her feet.

Clay could hear her in the background begging his father to reconsider.

"Wes, are you crazy? You can't do that to Clay, our boy!"

She continued frantically. She attempted to grab the phone and intercede, screeching at her husband with fear in her voice, "You can't do that to our son; who does that to his own son? What kind of father does that, calls the police on his own son?"

Clay could hear that she was crying. It broke his heart knowing how much he'd upset his mom. He knew how much she loved him. She tried to bite her tongue but the words continued to spill out. "I'm serious. I swear to God, Wes, I will never forgive you if you do such a thing."

Mr. Monning never wavered; though his heart was breaking, he knew that if he didn't get that kid home first, there was no telling what would happen to him. He had to get his boy home before somebody else got to him, even at the cost of filing a police report. Too many people would be looking for him, especially now. He'd rather Clay come home in the back of a squad car safe than picked up at the hospital. He didn't even want to think about that. If Clay wouldn't come home on his own, his father had no choice but to force his hand.

"Clay, please, I'm begging you, don't put me in this position. You have to come home. We have to deal with this mess that you're in."

Dead silence again. Clay fought back his own tears; but then the question came that nearly killed him.

"Son, why'd you do it?"

He didn't have an answer that sounded even halfway legitimate. He had a million excuses that at the time seemed reasonable, but now they seemed ridiculous, especially knowing the consequences of what had happened. He opened his mouth and tried to speak, but the words wouldn't come. Stuttering was the best that he could manage in the moment. His dad seized the opportunity to try and talk reason to him and give him one more chance to get home.

"Clay, despite what has happened, we're on your side. We love you and it doesn't matter why you did what you did, right now. It just has to be dealt with. You have to put this right, son. If you can't, then you can at least try. But in order to do that, you have to come home. We can help you. We'll do whatever it takes, but you've gotta come home."

Dead silence.

"Are you still there? Clay?"

"I'm here, Dad." It was clear that Clay was crying. His mom sobbed in the background.

"Dad . . . "

"Yes, son?"

"There's something I have to do and then I promise I'll come home."

"No! Come home first . . . please, I'm begging you." Despite his attempt to sound normal, Wes Monning's voice trembled with emotion.

"I can't, Dad. This is the hardest thing I've ever done, but I know I have to do this."

Dead silence.

"Dad, are you there?"

"I'm here, Clay."

"Dad?"

"What is it you think you have to do?"

The silence lasted for only a brief moment, but it felt like an eternity. Clay was shaking and rightfully so. His dad's nerves were on edge, knowing that his son should be at home. Marjorie

Monning was in tears, pulling at the phone, begging to talk to Clay. Wes shook his head no.

"Clay, please just come home."

"I can't, Dad. I have to talk to Mr. Granger."

"Mr. Granger? Mr. Granger? Who's Mr. Granger?"

"Mr. Granger is Greenlee's dad. I have to apologize to Greenlee and her dad."

Mr. Monning nearly dropped the phone. His instinct screamed that this was a terrible idea. It was simply too volatile a situation. This Mr. Granger wouldn't kill him, he supposed, but he could scare the hell out of him. Clay didn't stand a chance on his own, regardless of the explanation he'd try to deliver. Mr. Monning again tried to reason with him and asked if he could accompany him to talk to Mr. Granger. How had Clay gotten so off track right under his nose? He wondered how he could have failed his son so completely. He had no idea. But Clay needed him now and wouldn't accept his help.

"I'm not sure that's a good idea, son. In fact, I know it's not. I'll go with you." He took a deep breath and ran his fingers through his hair. "Clay, listen to me, please. I should definitely go with you. Come home and we'll go together. Clay—I respect you for taking responsibility for this mess. But going it alone is not the way to do it. Don't do it. I'm telling you, Clay, it's a mistake!"

Mrs. Monning grabbed the phone, crying. She begged her son to come home. "Clay, please, your father is right. Come home, for me. Please, Clay."

"I'm sorry, mom. I love you. Please give Dad the phone. Just let me talk to him."

With a tear-streaked face, reluctantly she handed her husband the phone and sank into a chair. Burying her hands into her face, she sobbed, knowing that her son was going to face the girl's parents alone. He could be facing charges and a father so angry that he might just kill him. Who knew what that boy of hers was about to walk into? They couldn't help him. What did that say about them? What had they done wrong? What had happened in Clay's world or Greenlee's, for that matter, to cause such a thing?

Clay's voice was trembling as he spoke to his dad. His battery was almost dead and though he could have recharged his phone, he didn't.

He spoke to his father one last time. "Please don't call the cops. Give me time to do what I need to do, and after that I promise I'll come home. If I don't, sir, then you can call them," and then Clay hung up the phone. *Click.*

His dad immediately called him back, but the phone had been turned off. Voice mail. He dialed again, as if this time his kid would pick up. Voice mail again. He left Clay a message on his third attempt; he didn't say what he really wanted to. Another wasted opportunity! The way Mr. Monning saw it, he had three options: wait for Clay to call back, pray that the kid would walk out of that house unharmed, or track down the Greenlee girl and against Clay's wishes meet him there.

"That's it," he yelled at the top of his voice. "We have to find out where she lives. We have to track down that girl!"

"What?" his wife said, stunned. "What did you just say?"

Suddenly, as if a light bulb went on, she jumped up from her chair and raced to the bottom of the stairs. At the top of her lungs she screamed for Claudia. Her daughter, not quite grasping the urgency of the situation, yelled from the top of the stairs. Frantic, her mother screamed again, and Clay's sister came running down the stairs.

"Slow down, Mom, please. I don't know what you're saying. Slow down."

Her mother grabbed her daughter's hands and said, "This Greenlee girl, *the girl*, we have to find her!"

Clay parked at the curb outside of Greenlee's house. Cars were parked in the driveway and the lights were on, but he couldn't tell who was home. Shaking his head, he turned off his truck and just sat there. He didn't dare step out of the vehicle just yet. Things he wanted to say rushed through his mind but none of them sounded right. He reworded them and even said them out loud, but they still sounded lame. Panicking, he started his truck, only to turn it off again, knowing he had to do this. He knew that it was now or never. Setting his jaw, he opened the door and stepped out into the cool night air. He was shaking, not because of the chill in the air, but because his nerves had taken over his entire body. He wished more than anything his dad was standing by his side. Why hadn't he let him come? He didn't know.

Putting one foot in front of the other, Clay made his way up the driveway to the front door. He couldn't breathe. His cheeks were flushed, his mouth dry, and his hands visibly shaking. Staring at the bell, he contemplated turning around and climbing back into his truck and driving until he hit a wall. His mother's smile flashed in front of his face, his father's hug engulfed his body, and his sister's laughter rang in his ears. He had no choice; he continued toward the door, stood on the mat, and rang the bell.

Chapter 26 - Let Me at Him!

Sally Granger was sitting on the couch, inconsolably sobbing. Matt Granger was pacing the floor, yelling at the top of his lungs. Greenlee, even with her head buried in her pillow, could hear them. Her own tears ran down her face, but her sobs were silent. She didn't dare let them hear her, knowing that they'd once again sit by her side and contribute to her pity party. Text after text blew up her phone, none worth reading, all degrading, and her voice mailbox was full. Marianne left messages but Greenlee didn't respond. Shaking, she wrapped a blanket around her, wishing it would all just go away. The chaos was interrupted by the erratic barking of her dogs at front the door. The yelling coming from the front room finally stopped and everyone wondered who could be at the door.

"I think there's someone at the door," Zoe, Greenlee's little sister, said.

She moved toward the front door, nudging the dogs out of the way as she did.

Opening it, she wasn't sure who the person standing on the doormat was. He seemed huge, at least to her. She didn't say anything at first, but then remembered her manners.

"Hi."

The boy appeared nervous, weird. His words did not come easily to him; mouth open, trying to speak, but nothing was coming out. Greenlee's sister spoke again.

"Are you okay?"

"Who is it?" Her father yelled from the front room.

The boy's eyes were huge. He pointed inside the hallway and asked a question that took Zoe by surprise.

"May I come in?" he asked.

Not sure what to do, she stepped back, opened the door wider and called for her dad.

"Dad, come here a minute."

He didn't come, but her mom did. Clay could tell she was a wreck: with red swollen eyes, she looked pitiful and he felt sick. She looked him straight in the face with a blank expression, as if she was unclear as to what she was supposed to say. Zoe once again took the lead.

"Mom, this guy asked to come in." She looked at him and then at her mom. "I don't really know what he wants, to be honest with you."

Mrs. Granger and Zoe looked at each other and then both turned and looked at Clay. He was visibly shaken. His brow had beads of sweat on it and he was wringing his hands in front of them. In fact, if Sally Granger wasn't mistaken, the kid seemed to be swaying back and forth.

"Are you okay?" Mrs. Granger asked. "You don't look well."

Clay shook his head, but then nodded. "I'm fine. No. I'm not fine. I'm sorry." He hesitated and then asked, "May I come in?"

Mrs. Granger stepped backward and pulled Zoe aside, allowing Clay entrance to the foyer. Mr. Granger suddenly appeared before them.

"Who's this?" he asked his wife.

She shrugged, not knowing herself. "I don't know, but I don't think he's well."

"Do you want me to call someone for you?" she asked, turning back toward Clay.

"What's your name? Do you need something?"

Clay's life ran through his head: mom, dad, sister, friends, teammates, and coaches. But then he did it. He announced his name. "I'm Clay Monning. May I speak to Mr. Granger please, and if at all possible, to Greenlee as well, ma'am?"

As soon as Mr. Granger heard the name, he lunged toward the boy. Mrs. Granger screamed, Greenlee's sister burst into tears, and Greenlee ran down the stairs as fast as she could, just as all hell broke loose.

"Let me at him!" roared Mr. Granger in a tone Greenlee had never heard in her life. "I'm going to kill him!"

Greenlee's eyes flashed and a piercing scream echoed in the hallway, but her dad paid no attention to what was taking place around him. Clay stood his ground, planted firmly in one spot, partially frozen with fear, and partly because he was trying to be a man. Mr. Granger was focused on one person: Clay Monning!

"No!" screamed Greenlee at the top of her lungs. "Dad, please, I'm begging you, stop! Please, just stop it."

Clay's eyes flashed toward Greenlee, briefly making eye contact. Mr. Granger suddenly blocked Clay's view as he stepped between him and Greenlee. Grabbing his collar with his other hand, he managed to pull Clay into the house and pinned him against the wall, but Clay still didn't fight back or try to protect himself. Mr. Granger screamed obscenities two inches from Clay's face. He didn't remember ever having said anything like that to anyone in his life. Beads of spit hit Clay's face, as the wrath of a father spewed onto his daughter's attacker, but Clay still held firm and took it. Every single thing that Mr. Granger screamed at him, Clay agreed with: he was scum, he was a dirt bag, he was cruel, he was evil, he was a disgrace. Clay agreed with it all.

Greenlee and her mom pleaded and begged for Matt Granger to stop. Zoe, horrified, had never seen her father so angry. She stood in one spot and screamed at the top of her lungs.

"Enough!" yelled Mr. Granger as he turned and stared at his family.

Stunned by his own actions, he smoothed back the hair from his face and turned to help Zoe, whose tears were streaming down her face.

"This is entirely your fault," he said to Clay. "Do you see what you have done?" He held his daughter in his arms for just a second, set her down on the stairs, then turned to face Clay.

"You've destroyed our family, you son of a bi—"

Before the words finished pouring out of his mouth and before his hand could land on the boy, another man burst through the door. He stood in front of Clay and raised his hands.

"With all due respect, I'm asking you to please lower your hand."

Mr. Granger moved Greenlee gently out of the way.

"Leave us now," he said to his girls. "You too," he told his wife.

"I'm not going anywhere, Dad. This concerns me," replied Greenlee.

Matt Granger pleaded with his wife. "She definitely doesn't need to be here," he said pointing to his youngest girl. "It's not right. Take her out of here."

His wife nodded and led her away. She looked back at Greenlee, but as soon as they made eye contact, Greenlee shook her head, and she knew that her daughter wasn't going anywhere.

"I take it that you're his father? What are you doing here?" Mr. Granger said with anger in his voice. "Haven't the actions of your son done enough damage? And then you burst into my home and upset my family more! You've destroyed my daughter. You've destroyed our family!" he said to both the Monnings.

Clay tried to speak but he couldn't. He was shaking and though he mouthed the words, they wouldn't come. He tried, but tears were flowing. He couldn't wipe them away quickly enough.

"I'm sorry. So sorry," was all he managed.

"Well, sorry is not going to cut it, now is it?" Mr. Granger's tone was bitter, cold.

Mr. Monning held up his hands in surrender. "I understand that we are all, all, in a terrible situation here," he said. "This has ruined everybody's life, especially your daughter's. There's no question that she has suffered the most, but this situation is a mess and as the adults, we have to be responsible and clean this up."

Matt Granger turned around and sat down on the stairs. He stared at Clay, a stupid boy who had destroyed his family for the sake of his ego.

"I know how angry you are with him," Mr. Monning said. "Hell, I want to kill him myself!"

Mr. Granger looked at Mr. Monning's exhausted face that was filled with anguish. The man that sat before him was not weak. He knew that he was a reasonable man and he had to be.

"Sir, I know how angry you are. God knows I am too, and I don't blame you." He took one step forward and continued. "That's my boy and yes, I'm disgusted with him. Hell, truth be told, I don't even recognize him right now! I'm furious with him, disappointed in him. I'm shocked by what has happened. Hell, I can't believe my boy would do that. I don't even know who he is right now." He hesitated, swallowed, and continued, "but he did it and there's no denying it." He took a deep breath and softened his voice. "But you see, I love my son like you love your daughter." His voice cracked and he wiped at his eyes. He continued though Clay recognized, as did Mr. Granger, that he was having difficulty.

"I don't know how to fix this, how to make amends for what has occurred between our two families."

Mr. Granger didn't speak for a few minutes, collecting his thoughts. Greenlee sat behind her dad, and though she wanted to, she didn't dare look at Clay. Clay didn't dare look at Greenlee, as he stood behind his father, who was partly blocking his view. Finally Mr. Granger spoke directly to Clay.

"I have never wanted to kill anyone in my life but I want to kill you for what you've done, it's true. I know I can't, but I still want to. I don't understand why you would do something so cruel to my daughter. It's incomprehensible to me, the damage that you have inflicted upon her, and for what? What? To gain acceptance? Or as a joke? Entertainment? It doesn't matter now, does it? The damage is done."

He stood up. He was pretty tall, thought Wes Monning. Greenlee stayed close, her arm wrapped around his, but listening to every word.

"Why'd you do it?" he asked Clay.

To everyone's surprise Mr. Monning stepped aside. "Answer him, son. I'd like to know, too, why? How could you do such a terrible thing?"

Clay stammered and wiped his eyes.

"Nooooo . . . don't." Mr. Monning clenched his lips, spoke softly, but said, "Cry over what you did, yes, but not the reason why. That was a choice. Tell us why you did such a terrible thing."

Every single little detail poured out of Clay's mouth. He struggled with his words and from time to time his dad patted him on his shoulder. Every now and then, he whispered for Clay to continue his story, encouraging him to finish. "You're doing fine son," he'd say.

Greenlee's tears flowed. Her father sat and shook his head from side to side and Mr. Monning stood stoically by his son. It was a touching, disheartening scene. Sally Granger listened from the top of the stairs and watched Greenlee, who was clearly embarrassed, finally excuse herself and step away.

"You've destroyed my girl. Do you know that?"

Clay nodded. "Yes, sir."

"For the sake of a *football* initiation, you've ruined her life." After a pause he continued, "Once this video went viral, it ruined her life." He cleared his throat. "She's only fourteen. These obscene pictures were faked, you knew it was faked."

Clay nodded, "Yes, sir."

Then Clay spoke confidently for the first time that evening.

"I know it makes no difference, but I swear on my life, I had no idea it was going viral. It was supposed to be a private, closed group, just between the guys for initiation only. Still wrong, dead wrong, and I'd give anything to take it back. But I swear about the video going viral, I had no idea it would ever go this far."

Mr. Monning shook his head and turned away from his son. His eyes closed and he took a deep breath, swallowed, and for the first time walked several feet away from Clay. He couldn't stand to be near him. Clay spoke again.

"It was supposed to be for me. It was my initiation, my deal. Not really Greenlee's."

"Not really Greenlee's!" Mr. Granger boomed. "Are you kidding me?"

Clay jumped and his head swung toward his dad, but Mr. Monning didn't move.

"I didn't mean it like that, sir. I swear. I meant, it was supposed to be on me. I was the one being initiated. Not Greenlee."

For some reason Laurel flashed through his mind: *The girls*, the competition between the two groups of girls, the jealousies, the adding of more people to the circle than the original team. It all got out of hand pretty quickly.

"It got out of hand."

"You think?" Greenlee had snuck back into the room and finally spoke, taking everyone by surprise. They all turned around and stared at her.

"*Out of hand?* That's what you're saying? You ruined my life!" She wiped her face with her sleeve. Her dad tried to put his arm around her but she shoved it off.

"You played me."

She wiped her face again.

"You played me, you jerk, in front of all of those people! My friends, my enemies, and all the people in between, my teachers included, hell, the whole world!"

"Greenlee, no need to talk like that!"

"Really, Dad!" she snapped.

"Well, maybe just this once!"

"I hate you Clay Monning! I really, really hate you!" Bursting into tears, she turned and ran up the stairs.

Wes Monning shook his head. His heart sank. "I don't blame her," he said heavily.

Clay was mortified.

Matt Granger rose up and stood two inches from Clay's face and stared into Clay's dark eyes. He watched Clay watch him.

"You are a lucky boy," he said.

They stood in the hallway eye to eye. "Everything inside of me wants to harm you in order to honor my child, my daughter, because I think she's owed that," he paused. "But I know hurting you doesn't help her and Clay, you are not worth anything to me." He turned and pointed to Mr. Monning. "But your well-being and safety are worth everything to him."

Clay stared at his dad. His heart jumped into his throat and the words "I'm so sorry, Dad" barely rolled off his tongue.

His dad blinked away his tears, nodded, and turned toward Mr. Granger, who was staring at the door, avoiding eye contact with Clay. Mr. Granger took a step backward and spoke firmly, but never looked in Clay's direction.

"Did you drive here?"

"Yes, sir."

"Get out, go home, and never return."

Mr. Monning nodded toward the door. Clay started to speak, but his dad shook his head *no*. Clay turned toward his dad, who was still planted in the hallway.

"Go on, Clay. I'll see you when I get home."

Wes Monning sent his son home. The air was thick with angry emotion. For a few moments, no one said a word. Mrs. Granger directed the men into the living room. They took a seat and she poured some coffee. The two men sat in silence, each lost in his own thoughts. They were startled when a tiny, shaky, voice broke the silence.

"I have something to say," Greenlee said. "It's my turn to speak."

Mrs. Granger jumped to her feet. "I'm not sure now's a good time, sweetheart. You've been through so much already."

Greenlee wasn't taking no for an answer. She walked with her head held high, stood in front of the three adults, and addressed them as if she'd planned this speech her whole life.

"This is my nightmare—mine! It sucks and it hurts, it's humiliating, and as of about fifteen minutes ago, I wanted to die." Her mother jumped to her feet, but Greenlee raised her hands and Mr. Granger pulled her back to the couch by her arm. "It's okay, I'm better now," she continued, with a confidence she didn't know that she possessed.

"I've never been so embarrassed in my life," she said, glancing at Mr. Monning. "I feel really stupid, because I really liked Clay and I thought he liked me." Her cheeks were red but she continued. Wes Monning swallowed the anger that burned in his gut, humiliated for his son and his family. Disbelief is what they all felt when Greenlee said what she did next.

"I'm not really sure Clay meant for this thing to get as bad as it did," Greenlee said and her mother gasped aloud.

"Don't get me wrong, it's bad, and I still hold him accountable, I do blame him. But I don't think he ever intended for it to get this bad." Her voice had softened and she looked so fragile that tears flowed down her mom's face.

"I think he's stupid, dumb, and I will never understand his reason, and that doesn't help me or anyone else that this could have happened to, but I'm ashamed that I was the one."

Matt Granger said in a fatherly tone, "Don't you say that. This is not your fault. You didn't do anything wrong."

Greenlee walked over and hugged her dad. He held her tight as her tears fell.

"It's his fault; it was his choice, and he chose to use you," her dad said quietly and Wes Monning cringed, knowing that he was right.

Greenlee wiped her eyes, stood back up, straight as an arrow, and continued to address the room.

"That really doesn't matter now, does it? It's gone viral. I've been called things you wouldn't dream your daughter would be called. That video is out there, and will haunt me for the rest of my life." She took a sip of water. "Clay's football scholarship chances are ruined. The other boys, they will never play at this school again. Charges could be pressed. Yes, *The Greenlee*

Project page has been taken down. Yes, the initiation was complete; but seriously, who won?"

All of the adults sat gazing appreciatively at Greenlee. Who was this girl? She was so mature for her age. The phone began ringing again and Sally Granger unplugged it just as Greenlee's little sister came down and snuggled next to her mother, confused and afraid. Greenlee wasn't finished. She had a plan. She'd had more than enough time to think: school, bedroom, and bathroom, she'd cried. Thought for hours. Felt angry, hurt, betrayed, all of those things, but then she felt as if she had two choices. Be the victim again or flip the situation and take back her self-respect. She wanted revenge at first, but now she had something better in mind. Something semi-positive, maybe, she hoped. Too much harm and damage had already been done. She wanted to put a positive spin on the entire situation, if that were even possible: more of an enlightening, an awakening, to help others, she had said. Her parents were curious about her idea, but thought that it might cause more damage to Greenlee. Mr. Monning sat in silence and waited to see where this was going.

"Think about this terrible situation," she'd said. "No one won here tonight. In fact everyone involved has lost something; and yes, I've lost the most." She flopped down into the armchair and wiped the tears from her eyes.

"Here's what I want to do," she stated. "I hope that you will help me with it, but I'm doing it anyway."

"What are you talking about, Greenlee? You realize that we are pressing charges; this is now a legal matter. The people involved have to be held responsible. We can't allow this to happen to anyone else."

Greenlee's eyes pleaded with her dad. "I'm begging you, Dad, no. You will only drag it out for me and ruin more lives. No more damage."

Mr. Monning's head shot up, and he looked appreciatively at Greenlee. This young lady was clever and strong. He waited in anticipation for Mr. Granger's response, praying that he'd listen to his daughter's reasons for not wanting to press charges, whatever they may be. Just listen to her! No football, no scholarship, that was one thing, but charges, that could mean prison. He didn't want Clay in jail.

"What are you talking about, baby? Please stop this nonsense. You're not thinking clearly. We've all had a big shock." He stood up but Greenlee raised her hands and motioned for him to sit back down.

"Greenlee, please." His voice was but a whisper. "I'm begging; make some sense, please."

"Dad, you're not thinking clearly," she said in response. "The damage done has been to me. I'm the one who's been hurt, me!"

There was something odd in her voice. Her father couldn't put his finger on it, and her mother had the same thought. They both had looks of bewilderment on their faces as they tried to make sense of what she was trying to say.

Mr. Monning sat perfectly still. His heart was pounding in his chest as he listened to Greenlee trying to reason with her parents. Was it even possible this kid would go to bat for his own kid after what he'd done? Surely not, but God, he hoped so!

"I think it's safe to say my life has been trashed! I'm being called a whore!"

Her father clenched his jaw, stretched his neck and anger filled his eyes. Mr. Monning's hopes of charges not being pressed seemed shattered.

Mrs. Granger put her hand on his arm. "Just listen to her, Matt."

"Like I was saying, I'm a joke. The joke's on me, they pulled it off, it was good!" She glanced at Mr. Monning, but he didn't dare look at her. "But that's my point. It doesn't matter that it's not true. If we press charges, this video will take on a life of its own. It will *never* go away." Taking a breath, she plopped down again, this time on the arm of a chair. "We, I, have the opportunity to do something right. I mean it when I say that I don't think Clay meant for it to get out of hand as bad as it did."

"You're wrong, Greenlee," her dad objected.

Mr. Monning sat silently.

"I think he was to blame, but I don't think he meant for it to go viral. I'm sorry; I just don't."

"And yet it did."

"Yes Dad, it did. But lots of lives have been ruined over this, not just mine. If we press charges we drag it back up, draw additional attention to the lies, and worse, ruin the lives of the families involved, and, Dad that is not *me*. That is not how the Grangers do things."

"What are you saying, exactly?" her mom asked. "Please tell us what you have in mind."

Greenlee cleared her throat as Mr. Monning held his breath. His son may not go to jail. Mr. and Mrs. Granger thought the stress had finally pushed their oldest daughter to the limit, especially when she dealt the final blow.

"I've had enough. I'm sick of all of it. We're going to handle this, but we're going to do it my way and Clay is going to assist." She turned to Mr. Monning. "You are going to make him do it, and he doesn't have a choice."

Mr. Monning nodded. He hadn't heard what she wanted him to do yet, but he was in no position to argue. Come hell or high water, his son would be there and would cooperate.

"Absolutely. What's your plan, Greenlee?"

"I'm going start a campaign with an open letter to the community. I agree that it's my job to make sure this never happens to anyone else ever again. We all seem to agree on that! But here's how we're going to do it!"

Chapter 27 - End It!

Greenlee's speech was heart-wrenching and there wasn't a dry eye in the room. Mr. Monning was so relieved and, try as he may, he couldn't contain his emotions any more. He jumped to his feet, ran to Greenlee, hugged her, and thanked her for her generosity of spirit. He had no control over the school board, coaches, students, or any parents' opinions for that matter, but Greenlee deciding not to press charges was huge! Her parents, despite disagreeing with her, supported her decision.

"There are no winners here," Greenlee stated. "The damage is done" was the statement that sealed the deal for her mother. It pierced her soul, stinging, because it was true.

"I'm the one who has been humiliated, called the names, made the fool, and these boys, though they made the choice to make me *The Greenlee Project*, I don't believe they meant for it to go viral. I don't think they realized how quickly they ruined my life with their ego-encased stupidity.

"It was wrong," she said, "we know that, but they'll never play football again here, or receive their football scholarships. They'll always be known as the scumbags that pulled off *The Greenlee Project*." She wasn't crying anymore. She spoke with strength, dignity, and confidence. She had their undivided attention.

"Their parents, families, and friends will continue to hurt, just like we are. They'll be humiliated and scorned because of what they did." She took a deep breath, exhaled, and continued. "Dad,

Mom, Mr. Monning, don't you see? We've all already paid the price."

Astounded by the speech she'd delivered with such proficiency, even Mr. Granger had no words. She spoke with such wisdom and conviction that they could hardly argue.

"My plan will make a difference. I will have my say about what they did and they will never be able to hold their heads high again." She glanced at Mr. Monning. "Plus, I believe my plan will help give me some kind of closure, if that's even possible. Does that even make sense?"

Mr. Granger spoke softly but addressed Mr. Monning. "I don't know if your boy deserves this kindness from my daughter, but when this is done, their paths will never cross again."

Mr. Monning sat in silence.

"But the fact that he came here tonight says something, at least to me. It says you did something right and maybe Greenlee has a point. I don't think so, not right now anyway, but maybe she does and I just can't see it yet. I admit, given the circumstances, it might take me a minute." He stood up and walked across the room and leaned on the mantel above the fireplace. "Let's say for argument's sake that these boys aren't all bad apples. What do we do? Their hands have already been dealt: no football, public scrutiny, scholarships out the window. What if that girl, standing right there," he pointed to his beautiful daughter, "is the only person in the world that still believes in the power of forgiveness?"

Mrs. Granger looked kindly upon her husband; his pain seared her heart as he spoke, shaken and broken, while he tried to understand a decision that his daughter had already made, one he didn't agree with.

"Greenlee has granted your son the gift of a lifetime. Don't let that monster of a son of yours blow it!"

Mr. Granger kissed Greenlee on top of the head, turned, and left the house. Greenlee walked to the front door, but her mother shook her head.

"Let him go. He needs some air and you need some rest."

Mr. Monning stood up, hands in his pocket, eyes looking down at the floor. "Greenlee, you name it. Tell me exactly what it is that you need, and my boy will get it done."

He glanced at Mrs. Granger. "I'll see myself out, ma'am. 'I'm sorry' doesn't begin to describe how I feel, though I'll say it on behalf of our family anyway. Greenlee, Mrs. Granger, I'm so terribly sorry," he said quietly and closed the front door behind him.

Clay had driven home, just like he'd been told, but he hadn't gone into the house. Parking his truck in the driveway, he went for a walk. The air had chilled considerably and he had pulled his hoodie over his head. Sick. He felt sick. The magnitude of the damage he'd inflicted upon Greenlee had suddenly hit him like a ton of bricks. He didn't feel sorry for himself, knowing he was the one in the wrong. How could he have been so stupid and cruel? She hadn't deserved such a thing, and he knew that! He'd started something that couldn't be repaired. He questioned whom he was and how on earth things had gotten so out of hand. Why did they get so caught up with something so cruel in the first place?

He found himself at the bus stop and climbed onto the first bus that pulled up. Sitting in a seat next to the window, his mind wandered. There was no fixing this, and he knew that. No way out. The disappointment in his father's eyes would haunt him forever. He'd never seen such a look on his father's face before. Feeling like a coward, he didn't have it in him to face his mother right then. He needed a minute to compose his thoughts, so much damage. But Clay knew that disappearing wasn't the answer. He got off at the next stop and started to walk back home. At least the walk gave him time to think, though the thoughts that raced through his mind just made him ill. His dad's face flashed through his mind. What would he say? How could he make it up to him? His dad's dreams for him were gone, and knowing that his dad had come to his defense at Greenlee's house made Clay question everything all over again.

His mother was waiting for him outside the door, phone in her hand. She ran toward him and hugged him as if she hadn't seen him in years.

"Clay," was all she said.

"Is Dad back?" he asked.

She shook her head and wrapped her arm around his shoulder, and led him into the house.

Clay went up the stairs without saying a word. Flopping onto his bed, he closed his eyes. Sleep never came. He waited until he heard his father come through the front door. Too nervous to move, he held his breath. Maybe his dad might come up to talk or lecture him. He didn't. This was worse. The silence was a torture he couldn't stand. If he'd been yelled at, it would be over by now. Silence equaled disappointment and Clay didn't know what to do. A wave of nausea swept over him. He ran to the bathroom and threw up. His sister handed him a cool washrag. Not saying a word, she put a blanket on the floor, turned, and walked away. Clay spent the evening right by the commode. Face down. At one point, his dad put a blanket over him, but didn't stay. Any other time, in such a state, he would have sat with him or helped him move to his bed. Not tonight. His boy was on his own. The next morning he was awoken bright and early, told to shower and forced to eat a piece of toast and to sip a clear soda.

"What's going on?" he said so softly. "It's Saturday, and I don't have practice. What's going on?"

"You're going to the Grangers'," his mother answered.

"What?" he asked her to repeat that.

"You heard me, the Grangers'. You're going over there." She poured another cup of coffee for herself. "You have work to do!"

Chapter 28 - Closure

Mr. Monning hand-delivered Clay. The scene in the kitchen at the Grangers' was awkward, at best. Clay nervously fidgeted with his laptop. Pen and paper had been provided for taking notes. He politely declined refreshments, and Mrs. Granger didn't push them too hard. Mr. Granger scowled at her for even offering.

Greenlee finally appeared in the doorway. Her heart sank as she looked across the table and saw Clay's face. He still got to her—no change there. She hated herself for that and tried really hard not to look at him.

"Let's end this," she said. "Once and for all; if we're lucky, we'll prevent anyone else from going through this again and we'll put an end to what they're saying about me."

Clay started to speak but the frog in his throat prevented him from talking without clearing it first. Greenlee actually found that amusing, though she managed to keep a solemn face, which made him squirm in his seat.

"May I say, Greenlee, I'm so sorry and if I could take it all back I would."

At first she didn't respond. He cleared his throat again.

"Don't, please," she said, finally.

Sitting at the table she organized her stuff, placing her laptop in front of her, notebook to her left, pens to the right, and a bottle of water on the floor to her left. For some reason Clay noticed these things. Turning her laptop on, she opened up a blank document, and finally gave him instructions.

"A letter. We're going to write open letters—essays—and send them to the newspapers, school officials, parents, and students. In fact, we're going to send them to anyone who will read and post them." She took a sip of water. "Oh yeah, they're apology letters. Well, yours is. Mine will be in regards to why I'm not pressing charges against you and your vile friends. Do you have any questions?"

She didn't stop what she was doing and had already started outlining what she thought she might say. Clay's face was blank, as was his outline. He hadn't anticipated writing an open letter, but he wasn't about to argue. He did have a question, though.

"What do you think mine should really address. I mean, what we did or why we did it? Or why we wished we hadn't?"

Greenlee pondered the question before she answered. It was actually a good question.

"I think it should encompass all three. This is about helping others. Write it straight from your heart. You know, actually *heartfelt*. How about that? So what would you say to others regarding this situation?"

He nodded. He got it. He agreed with her, actually; it could help bring him closure too, though he wouldn't dare breathe that.

Her voice was soft. "If we're lucky we'll both find some peace and closure and prevent this from ever happening to anyone else ever again."

He agreed. "Sounds like a good plan, and once again, I'm so sorry."

"Let's get on with it then," she said. "If we're lucky . . . luck's the wrong word. If we're *successful*, we'll make a difference."

Greenlee's Open Letter:

Hello:

My name is Greenlee Lynn Granger. I'm a teenager, a high school student, but unfortunately, due to recent events, many of you know me as "The Greenlee Project." I've tried really hard to be a good daughter, friend, sister (though I'm not always good at that), and person. I had no idea that the day I'd fallen for the new kid, the cutest boy in school, would end up being the worst experience of my life. It was then that I became the biggest joke of the entire school! Being his initiation project was bad enough, but being an entire "public" joke was, as you can imagine, absolutely brutal.

I won't bore you with the details. If you'd like to view actual footage, please go to www.utbville.com or www.gotfootageposthere. To my dismay, there are copies available for your viewing entertainment. Trust me, I know. We can't seem to remove them, though we've tried. Naturally my family and I are horrified and disgusted by this, but they keep appearing. We're tired of fighting it. For the record: **THESE VIDEOS ARE FAKE. NICE JOB, BUT FAKE ALL THE SAME!!!!!!** I have chosen not to allow them to ruin my life. As you can imagine, this wasn't an easy choice for me, and it's safe to say it took me a while to come to this decision.

What did this do to my family and me?

Clearly humiliation tops the list! Devastation, of course, betrayal—it's been bitter and heartbreaking. The stress has gone beyond my family's wildest tolerance levels. During the project, my feelings were cast aside, as if I were worthless and meaningless. Every conversation that I'd ever had with the boy I liked was recorded and replayed for everyone else's daily amusement. My honest feelings meant nothing, and knowing that I was played embarrassed and humiliated me. I can only imagine how it must feel to be my parents.

Surely a girl as smart as me should have known better, right? Not so. I honestly didn't have a clue! How sad is that? I will bear this humiliation, as will my family, for the rest of our lives. I have been called every name in the book, whore, slut, ho, TGP, etc.! And the photos of me and the faked video that went viral, well, as you can see, it is still out there. My reputation is toast, and my parents and sister, well—they suffer with me. Yes, the initiation joke was successful—and because of that I a—no, we have been—

destroyed. The devastation has wiped out our family emotionally, yes, but it has destroyed the other families involved as well, and those are the ones I'd like you to also consider.

*I'm certain most of you will not understand what I'm about to say. Please bear with me, and for the sake of the innocent family members, try to understand where I am coming from. *

The boys involved in this mess have been punished. They are great athletes, smart students, and as far as I know, they've never been in trouble before. These boys will never play football again, **at least not at this school**. Their scholarships are gone, and their families are humiliated by their actions. **I don't think they meant this initiation to get so out of hand.** As shocking as this may seem, coming from me, **I truly believe THEY DID NOT MEAN FOR THE VIDEO OR THE GREENLEE PROJECT TO GO VIRAL! I DO NOT BELIEVE the team, including Clay Monning, would have made that decision, posting the video on the INTERNET. Regarding this issue, they are victims of technology too. They have already been punished for the idea of The Greenlee Project. I do not believe that they should continue to be persecuted, and neither should I.** However, what they did is unacceptable and must never happen again! The damage is extensive, but it is done. They hurt me, and my family, BUT the malicious act of posting the video wasn't a team decision. One mean person is responsible for that part!

Please understand, I do not under any circumstances justify "The Greenlee Project." I just cannot in good conscience condemn the families associated with the actions of these people. The suffering we've endured has been too much already. I believe, based on the past history of these kids, and **it pains my family for me to say this,** that these boys deserve another chance. **If they find the kid(s) that posted the actual video, that kid(s), should be dealt with individually**.

It is for this reason I hope the punishment that they've already received will suffice. **I'm asking you, as is my family, that you allow these boys to continue with their studies.** Please do not insist additional charges be pressed. I will not press charges nor will I testify against the team: (1) I can't bear the thought of a trial and additional humiliation, and (2) I don't believe that their parents deserve to suffer for their sons' stupidity. **Though my parents are struggling with my decision, they have opted to back me.** I am asking that you do the same. **I would like to put this behind me. Yes . . . I know . . . I AM Greenlee Lynn Granger. I am THE GREENLEE PROJECT. But I am not who the people that posted comments say I am.** By the way, my parents are on the fence with this letter. They are good people, but they are struggling with my decision and they are hurt by the events that have taken place.

Greenlee Lynn Granger

Clay's Open Letter

My name is Clay Monning and I'm an idiot!

I can't believe that the activity that I participated in, of my own accord, was in order to achieve the acceptance of my teammates. What should have been a simple initiation turned into a cruel joke that ruined multiple lives.

I've let down so many people that I care about: my dad, my mom, sister, coaches, teammates, friends, and most of all Greenlee Lynn Granger. I'm ashamed of my actions and take full responsibility for my behavior. I kept pushing the envelope in order to pull off the greatest initiation our team had ever seen. It was the worst initiation in the history of our school. It's safe to say I don't even recognize myself when I look into the mirror. My reflection looking back at me—I don't know who that is.

The Greenlee Project was a monstrous act that turned into something more horrendous than I could have imagined. I'd give anything for us, the team, not to have participated in this horrific act. I take full responsibility for the project and wish I could take it all back, but I know that I can't. Saying sorry isn't enough, but I truly am! We all are! I hope that no one else does anything so stupid. None of it was worth it! The initiation quickly got out of hand, and we couldn't control the environment that we'd set up. It snowballed and ran away from us. This does not, by any means, justify what we did. I am telling you that not a single member of our team is proud of this malicious act.

I'm ashamed of what I've done, and I'm not proud that others think a project of such monstrous acts was a success because a team pulled it off. It was not a success! I am fully aware of the damage I have instilled upon this family, my family, and those around me. The disappointment that I have caused is too much to bear; my dad can't even look at me, and my mom is ill at my sight.

I want everyone to know how badly I hurt an innocent girl, Greenlee Granger. It wasn't her fault and she was innocent of everything. Everything that is out there on the net is FAKE. All of it was a SETUP, MANIPULATED AND ARRANGED. SHE IS INNOCENT OF EVERYTHING. It was a terrible thing that we participated in, and it will truly haunt me forever. I can hardly sit across this table (we're writing these letters together), without seeing the pain that I've caused reflected in her eyes. It makes me sick, as it should! I knew better than to do this! I was raised to be a better man than the way I have acted. I'm grateful that I'm even here with her today to write this letter to you (our community), though I know I don't deserve this opportunity.

I have no idea why Greenlee would try to help us, me, my family, and the other guys involved, but I'm glad that she is. We are undeserving of this act of kindness and that's for sure! I will try really hard to make it right, though I'm not sure how, but I'll make it right if it takes me the rest of my life! I have no idea what this community will demand of me, but if you follow Greenlee's suggestion, then it truly will be a gift of forgiveness. I will leave it up to you; I have no words left except for the following public apology:

Though sorry is not enough, I am. I mean it, truly. I'm sorry Greenlee! Please, forgive me. I was selfish and wrong. I will truly regret this for the rest of my life. I don't want to be that kind of man.

Clay Monning

Both letters appeared in the local paper and the school paper. They also went viral on the Internet, were carried on the local news, and even had a spotlight on the national news stations. Greenlee, Clay, and their families appeared on several late-night talk shows, and though Greenlee refused to discuss the actual acts that took place during *The Greenlee Project*, both kids discussed why cyberbullying is so harmful to teens. Town-hall meetings took place in their town, which spread across the country. The school board met, and though certain officials tried to press charges against the kids on the team, they were faced with opposition from Greenlee and against their will, her family. The police had trouble locating the kids that posted the actual video, but were still searching for them during the town-hall meetings and media frenzy that took place. The investigation continues.

The boys on the team that were actively involved weren't allowed to play football for the rest of the season. Underclassmen were placed on probation for the following year, but seniors were out of luck: they sat out their senior year and scholarship chances were pulled. Official legal charges were dropped due to the fact that Greenlee refused to press them or testify. Mr. Granger still struggles with Greenlee's decision but is proud of the maturity that she showed, and the work that she has accomplished in order to help other teens avoid becoming victims of cyberbullying.

Wes Monning, grateful for his son's second chance, worked with the Grangers spending hours at local rec centers mentoring local teens. They discussed bullying, cyberbullying in particular, initiations, and the damage of today's technology if used carelessly or maliciously. Clay, though he is forbidden to play football, discussed the perils of cruel and harmful initiations with new players, and has spoken twice during pep rallies.

Greenlee and Clay partnered and spoke to thousands of kids across the country, speaking about cyberbullying to thousands of teens at conferences, youth groups, and high schools. Greenlee received a writing scholarship to a wonderful university based upon her open letter, community work, and the speeches that she continued to give across the country. She became the face of

The Greenlee Project; but this time the project had a brand-new look. It became a massive teen movement, based on educating teens about the damaging effects of cyberbullying. Clay assisted, but took a back seat. He continued to train in the gym in the hopes of one day setting foot on the football field again.

Laurel and her BFFs accepted zero blame. Greenlee felt nothing but pity for such a selfish, shallow person, and supposed that Laurel would never change.

Discussion questions from *The Greenlee Project*, a fictional book with real-life experiences, provides an opportunity for teens and tweens to discuss their lives and issues that are happening around them. These discussion questions are an outlet for teens and tweens to understand more about how actions have consequences and how decisions can impact others, good and bad.

1. What character did you identify with and why?

2. Do you think Greenlee is at fault for anything that happened in TGP?

   o   If yes, why?
   o   If no, why not?

3. Do you think Clay, or any of the other characters in the book that were involved with TGP, should have had legal charges brought against them?

   o   If no, why not?
   o   If yes, who?

4. Do you think the suspension from football for the year was punishment enough from the school?

5. Are there situations in TGP that are similar to real-life situations that you know about?

6. What other ending(s) could this book have had?

7. What do you think Clay regrets the most?

8. What other choices and decisions did the football team and other students make that caused Greenlee to feel so humiliated?

9. Do you think Laurel and her friends should have had to face some consequences?

10. How did social media factor into the story and outcome?

11. What concerns do you have about social media in the world you live in?

12. Can you recognize a cyberbully?

Acknowledgement

I would like to thank my family for their patience, and my business partner and friend, Jan, for her support. Anne Dunigan, my content editor, mentor, and friend, whose insight, advice, and business knowledge has never failed me. "Thank you!"

To those that spent time with me and assisted during my research while writing this book, thank you for your time and patience. A special thank you to Lisa Robinson and Donnie Light, you know what we've been through with this book!

I hope we can help at least one tween or teen, if not more, with the message in this book. Some of these scenes were difficult to write: especially knowing my girls are at this vulnerable age, a preteen and a teenager. I hope they are never victims of such bullying nor participate in such terrible acts.

Krista, Lauren, and Zack, I love you!

About the Author

Author Photo Credit: Jessica Prigg
Modern Studios Photography

Born in England, moved to Texas and resides there still. Author of several children's books including picture books, middle-grade chapter books, YA and a reader's theater titled *What If... A Story of Shattered Lives*. Amanda conducts workshops, writes a blog, contributes to an online magazine and shares her writing process and what she has learned as a publisher with people of all ages. As Chief Executive Officer of Progressive Rising Phoenix Press, she assists authors with their work. A recipient of the Mom's Choice Awards, she continues to write. Works in progress include the third installment of the Mischief series and two adult novels.

The Mom's Choice Awards® (MCA) evaluates products and services created for parents and educators and is globally recognized for establishing the benchmark of excellence in family-friendly media, products and services. Using a rigorous evaluation process, entries are scored on a number of elements including production quality, design, educational value, entertainment value, originality, appeal and cost. Around the world, parents, educators, retailers and members of the media trust the MCA Honoring Excellence seal when selecting quality products and services for families and children.

www.amandamthrasher.com

www.progressiverisingphoenix.com

Also by Amanda M. Thrasher

The Ghost of Whispering Willow

Mischief in the Mushroom Patch

A Fairy Match in the Mushroom Patch

Sadie's Fairy Tea Party

What If... A Story of Shattered Lives

There's a Gator Under my Bed!